Homebodies

Cheryl Loudermelt

Idyll Owl Books
875 S. Estrella Pkwy #6882
Goodyear, AZ 85338
www.idyllowl.com

Published by Idyll Owl Books 2018

Cover Art by Eva van Ginhoven

ISBN: (Paperback)   978-1-949089-03-5
          (eBook)   978-1-949089-02-8

For Candy

Homebodies

Todd got home at five-fifteen, and because Emily knew Todd was ridiculously routine, her daily irritation began promptly at five-sixteen, one minute after Todd kissed her forehead, threw in a DVD he'd seen a hundred times, and flopped down on the sofa while he waited on her to finish cooking dinner. Part of her, a very small part, thought she shouldn't be so frustrated with him because he did go to work every day and was probably tired when he got home, but the other, much larger part felt like thwacking him soundly on the back of the head with the nearest pan.

Irritation was her default mood for cooking anything, a small stubborn piece of her brain getting things done, and a much larger, irritable piece messing everything up by distracting her with thoughts of skull smacking. It didn't help that Todd had a huge cowlick directly at the crown of his head. It was like he came preinstalled with a frying pan target because God knew he was going to be a pain.

Since she found it impossible to keep her mind in the kitchen, Emily was a miserable cook. Time failed to improve her abilities. She could make the same recipe seven hundred times and still not increase her chances of it coming out any better. Someone, she couldn't remember who, had once told her the key to good cooking was to make everything with love, but Todd was just lucky she didn't spit in the food. To his credit, Todd never complained no matter how bad it was. She wasn't sure if that decision was an act of kindness on his part or if he had reasonably good survival instincts that told him he'd probably lose his head if he commented on how dry the meat was. Whatever the reason, each day she made dinner, she remembered that Todd never complained, and the small stubborn part that managed remotely edible food would swell just enough to hold back the fury of the frying pan. And eventually, they could sit together and eat, both still conscious and unbroken, at least on a good day.

This was not a good day. She was in danger of losing both the product of her labor and her self-control. The potatoes were about to boil over, the sauce was trying hard to burn on the bottom, the meat needed to be turned before it charred in the skillet, and she only had two hands and enough skill to handle one of these problems at a time. She did the reasonable thing and called for Todd to help her in the kitchen, and he did the completely unreasonable thing she expected him to do because he was so infallibly routine.

"I'll be there in a minute." He called from the living room, and then laughed at some stupid part of that ridiculous movie he couldn't possibly still enjoy after seeing it so many times. She imagined his face smiling. He always started out handsome. He kept in shape, which was nice, and he was very tall with soft green eyes and a wide mouth that added something extra to his happiness. But all of that was ruined after an hour or two of his company when the beauty of him shattered and all that remained was a grating feeling, like having broken glass in every pore.

She was at least four hands short of getting dinner on without destroying it, but she wished for a fifth hand and a long arm to beat him with the heavy iron skillet they only used for tortillas and cornbread. The potatoes boiled over at least five minutes before Todd got off the sofa, and the meat was black on one side and filling the kitchen with smoke. She managed to save the sauce. Little victories, she told herself, mostly to keep from bonking him.

"What can I do?" Todd asked, watching her frantically trying to salvage dinner as though she were some odd zoo creature who didn't know how to use human things.

"There's nothing left to do now but eat burnt food. I needed you five minutes ago." She tried and failed to keep coldness from her voice. She was all out of little victories that day.

"It wasn't five minutes."

Todd rolled his eyes at her, clearly unaware of how close his forehead was to impacting the bottom of a hot pan. "It might have been six."

"Don't exaggerate. I swear it is physically impossible for you to cook something without wrecking the kitchen." There was a bemused tone to his voice that did not decrease her desire to thump him with a blunt object. "What's that all over everything?"

"Potatoes." She managed through clenched teeth. "I'm making mashed potatoes."

"Were you planning on mashing them directly on the stove?"

"Yes, Todd. I only called you in here to admire my masterful technique of mashing potatoes directly on the stove." She might have not had the extra hand to slug him with, so she threw pots and pans with both eyes.

Todd took a step back and smiled his bomb-diffusing smile. "I like mashed potatoes, no matter how you want to make them. What else have you got?"

She stared down at the meat still smoking in the pan. Every day he asked her what she was making she felt an odd distance, like the floor had become another foot further away. "Uh. Blackened pork chops, I guess."

"It almost sounds like you meant to do that."

"Yeah. I asked for you to come help so you could admire that too." If she wasn't careful, all the food was going to taste like sarcasm, because she was slopping it all over the kitchen.

He nodded, still grinning at her. "It looks like you've got things under control."

Like some magical dinner imp, he disappeared into the other room, leaving her to not only finish dinner, but clean up the mess too. She did the cleaning first, both so the sticky parts wouldn't have time to dry on everything, but also so Todd's food would be cold. She had one more little victory after all.

She also left the cabinet doors open because she was short enough to walk under them, but he was tall enough to smash into them with his face and generally not situationally aware enough to avoid that trap before it was too late. By the time they sat down to dinner, Emily had eaten enough vexation to feel full. She stared at her plate, disgusted with its contents, and then around the room so she didn't have to look at Todd.

Their house had two living rooms, one was supposed to be a formal room for company, but since they never had company inside the house, it was little more than a mausoleum to Crate and Barrel. The kitchen divided the formal area from the family room, which probably she should really call the couple room since they weren't large enough to constitute a whole family; it had both the dining room table and their sofa, which was very large and had a chaise on each end. When they'd bought it, Todd hadn't known what the hell a chaise was. He just called it the feet thing, which was funny at the time, but getting old. Their dining room table was large too, with cushy blue chairs that would seat eight people with ease. It was ridiculous how much extra space they had for two people, but they needed the ridiculous furniture to fill up the ludicrous house, so they could be just as foolish as everyone else on the street. She poked at the burnt meat with a fork prong. It was so stiff she could have used it as a doorstop.

Todd said exactly nothing, which was either very smart or exceedingly stupid, but she didn't have the energy to figure out which and still maintain the intensity of concentration it took to shuffle lumpy mashed potatoes around her plate. Eventually, she lost the will for that too and left the potatoes in a misshapen little glob.

"Not hungry?" Todd sawed at his meat in a way slightly reminiscent of a lumberjack. "You don't eat enough."

"I have lost weight." It was starting to be a struggle to keep jeans above her hips. "I used to think that was a good thing."

"So, eat more. Eat whatever you want for a few days. I'll stop and get you chocolate." Getting chocolate was Todd's way of soothing every argument, and she was beginning to associate the taste with being angry with him.

"I don't want chocolate."

He set his fork and knife down beside his plate. "What do you want?"

Sometimes even his patience was enough to make her livid. "Not this and not chocolate. At this point, new jeans would probably be easier." She stood up from the table and scooped her dirty silverware onto the plate.

"Where are you going?"

"Nowhere. I just don't want to eat." After she scraped the better portion of her dinner into the garbage and put her plate in the sink, she couldn't bring herself to go back in the room with Todd. He would make her talk when she didn't feel like talking, and when she did feel like talking he would pretend that she had nothing to say. Instead, she went into their formal room to wander aimlessly until Todd was done eating, and she could finish the dishes.

She had no hope that Todd would do the dishes. Dishes were not a thing Todd did, and she was pretty sure that he either didn't know how to wash dishes, or that he was completely convinced a mystical dish fairy took care of that task, meaning his exertion in that arena was never required. She tried to remember that Todd did other things. He went to work every day and never mentioned her getting a job or something even though their house and half a dozen credit cards always kept them in debt. He washed the cars and changed their oil and tires, and he fixed anything in the house that was broken.

Most things. There were some things he refused to work on, like more effective communication or empathizing with her less logical emotions. Everything else was in working order, but sometimes it was better if they didn't speak. She heard the soft reverberation of his footsteps in the kitchen, his plate slide onto the counter, and then his retreat into the other room to watch his movie.

Emily closed her eyes to blink away the nuisance of mildly homicidal images and went to the window. She was proud of the formal room from a decorative standpoint. Everything was soft yellow and grey, with little pops of teal that tied everything together. It looked like the kind of room printed in a magazine, except she bought everything on clearance and had to do some of the work herself. Still, that room always felt a little suffocated because of the boards on the windows. Even though she'd painted them to match the room, she did wish sometimes that she could add a bit of yellow sun to the other shades of yellow there. The boards were Todd's idea, and even though she didn't like them, she thought that he should have some say so about the way their house looked since he had to live there too. They'd compromised in leaving little spaces between the boards, so that she could peer between them and into the front yard. It was dark; the streetlights hadn't worked in ages, but she pulled back one of the curtains anyway to look out on the grass.

Immediately, she groaned and could not stop the annoyed eye roll that was determined to happen even without her consent. Brown and bloodshot eyes stared back at her from the front yard. She sighed and waved. "Hello, Mr. Turlington."

Mr. Turlington growled, and a bubble of tar-like drool formed at the corner of his mouth. The veins in his forehead were black and raised above his grey skin. "I assume you're here about the landscaping again. Wait here a tick while I grab Todd."

She closed the curtain in a manner that was more like slamming the door in Alan Turlington's face. He was the kind of guy who she was sure didn't own a single pair of pants that weren't khakis. It was the only color in the world, apparently, and at any given time, he looked like he was preparing to depart on a private boat excursion, except that he didn't own a boat, unless she counted the one he floated on in the sea of pretentiousness that flowed from his every cell. He had been the head of the homeowner's association for as long as they'd lived there, and he was always bitching about the landscaping. Their homeowner's association rules clearly said that weeds could reach a maximum height of six inches, and she pulled them practically every day, but Turlington just had to complain about something because he was a jerk and wasn't content unless he had landscaping to bitch about and homeowners to harass. He'd been driving them crazy since they bought the house. She couldn't remember how long it had been.

"Todd." Her voice was quiet but seething. "Mr. Turlington is in the yard again."

"Christ." Todd rolled his eyes and reached beside the sofa for the shotgun he carried to and from work. "I'll take care of it in a minute."

Emily stood in the doorway, her hands shaking because they couldn't reach out and strangle him. Todd's eyes didn't waiver from the television. Sometimes she felt like she could cut off a hand, and he'd put off getting her a towel long enough for her to bleed out. "Give me the shotgun, Todd."

"I said I'd do it in a minute." He wasn't upset, which only made her more agitated. Sometimes, she was certain he told her that he would do things in a minute, so she would be impatient and do them before he had a chance.

"I know you did, but you're clearly very interested in this movie, still, after having seen it so many times, and Mr. Turlington is being polite enough to wait before chewing us out today, so give me the shotgun. I'll take care of him."

"Okay." Todd pulled his eyes from the T.V. for a split second to glance at her face, which Emily knew was painted with an expression that could leave no doubt of her mood. If he saw, if he cared, he said nothing, and handed over the shotgun. "You have to take the safety off. It's that button on the side."

She jerked the shotgun out of his hand. "I know how to work the shotgun, Todd." Emily marched into the formal room again, muttering to herself that she knew how to work the stove, and the dishwasher, and the mop, and the guns. She knew how to work the door locks, which she wrenched open so hard she was momentarily grateful she didn't jerk them right out of the door. She could take care of Mr. Turlington. She could always take care of things because she always had to take care of things, because sometimes the only things Todd knew how to work were the DVD player and the buttons he could push to piss her off. "Todd's busy, Mr. Turlington." She smiled in the most neighborly way she could muster. "I guess it's just you and me."

Mr. Turlington reached out an arm and clawed the air with black fingernails. A soft moan drifted across the pristine lawn.

"I know." She said, raising the shotgun. "Todd just works so much. I try to do it in the mornings, but I'm sure you understand there's more to life than yard work."

Mr. Turlington took a step forward, unsteady on his feet because one of his legs had been partially chewed through his khakis. Another moan.

"We do the best we can." Emily pressed the safety. Red for dead. Did Todd really think she couldn't understand something as basic as that? It even rhymed for Christ sake. She pulled the shotgun into the pocket of her shoulder and leveled it at Mr. Turlington's head. She was pretty sure he dyed his hair to match his pants. "I promise. I'll get on it first thing in the morning."

She pulled the trigger. There was a boom, a mist of red and black, a splatter, and some of Mr. Turlington ended up in the bushes and dripping from the leaves. The rest of him fell, the thump muted by their thick green grass. The first thing she did was spray off the bushes with the water hose. The last thing Mr. Turlington would want would be to muck up the landscaping.

"You have a good night. Mr. Turlington. Say hello to Brian for us." She put the safety on and went into the garage for a shovel. She would bury him next to Brian, his son. She thought that's where he would want to be, and there were some lovely unkempt bushes nearby.

Then alone, she dragged Mr. Turlington's body to the empty lot at the end of the street where they put all the neighbors who came into the yard too often. She didn't ask Todd to help. He'd only make her wait.

2

It was several hours before Emily made it in to finish the dishes, and by then, she was too tired to be angry anymore. She washed them as loudly as possible, but Todd had moved on to another movie and made no move to come and help her.

She was wrong to hope for it. She was wrong to hope for anything, really. People had to stop growing eventually. Everything became stagnant and slowed to a crawl. At this point, their marriage was what it was going to be, and it wasn't perfect, but it was nominally functional, and that was probably the best it would ever get for either of them.

He didn't show it of course, but Todd wasn't any happier with her than she was with him. She was almost never in the mood for sex, and when they had sex it was boring. Todd needed someone who was laid back, but he'd married her, and she was a little high strung. She wondered why they stayed together and thought that maybe the thing they had most in common was their doleful acceptance of something that was marginally good enough.

14

By the time she finished the dishes, dried her hands, and went to sit with him on the sofa, she had exhausted her way to inner peace. Being angry and getting over it might be the closest thing they had to real love. She watched him sitting on the sofa, three cushions, and miles away, and wondered if he noticed the difference in her mood between the crappy DVDs.

Todd had the worst taste and a collection to rival all humanity. He preferred comedies, not ones that were remotely intelligent or satirical, but the kind that relied heavily on fart jokes and sexual innuendo. She could never understand why he found gas so hysterical, and while she appreciated the effort at humor, she just wasn't made to measure the subtle shades of comedic difference between letting one rip and cutting the cheese. After about thirty minutes of marital silence punctuated by only theatrical flatulence, she was ready to shut down for the day.

"I'm going to bed, Todd."

He glanced at her but turned his head back to the television. She only caught half his frown. "It's so early."

She bit down on her bottom lip to prevent it from saying anything before she had time to think about it. "I don't know if you noticed, since you didn't bother to ask, but I'm not exactly having the best day."

Todd gave her another glance that flashed

about as quickly as a guy naked beneath an overcoat. "What happened?"

Emily thought if someone had looked in from the outside, they would have assumed Todd was talking to the characters in his movie. If she really wanted to get his attention she was either going to have to strip or learn some jokes about farting. Neither of those things would happen before bedtime. "Nothing. Nothing at all Todd. I worked in the garden by myself. I made dinner by myself. I shot Mr. Turlington, dragged him down the street, and buried him by myself, and now I'm going to bed by myself. It was a perfectly normal, absolutely ordinary day."

Todd looked at her long enough to roll his eyes. "Why are you complaining about things going the way they are supposed to go? Normal is a good thing."

"Normal is just normal, I mean, neutral, but. . ." He was only listening with half his brain. He may have only possessed half a brain some days, but she couldn't prove it without an MRI. "I'm not complaining. I'm going to bed."

"You want me to go with you?" He looked straight at the television, which meant he was offering to do something he didn't want or plan to do.

"No."

He jumped on his good fortune quicker than he'd jumped on anything else that day.

"Okay. Goodnight."

She let out a measured sigh, steam to depressurize. "Goodnight."

Expectation was her enemy. She thought it might have always been, but she couldn't really remember. What did it say about them that her brain didn't find memories of them worth saving? She shuffled to the stairs and stood there, staring at the carpet, trying to think of one single thing about them that didn't seem so mundane it might bring her a pang of happiness. When that failed, she looked up the stairs and tried to find something to make her angry instead, but even that was useless. There wasn't happiness, there wasn't sadness, there was just ordinary. Maybe he was right. Maybe she was just complaining about things going well. They didn't really know any other married couples. She had very little basis for comparison.

Their house was perfect. She remembered buying it, being happy, and she remembered picking out the curtains and carpets, and hanging that floral wreath. She remembered Todd boarding up the windows and adding that additional lock on the front door. She remembered Pottery Barn, but she couldn't remember what all of it was for.

Every house on their street looked the same on the outside, but they all couldn't be so alienated behind closed doors. She and Todd had gotten their own piece of the cookie cutter, and she'd decorated the cookie how she'd always wanted. It was perfect, flawless, and meaningless. They only really used the living room and the kitchen, and one of the four bedrooms to sleep in. Their lives were useless space filled with useless things that didn't make them happy any more than it made them whole.

She stared up the stairs, at the white door at the top; she couldn't remember the last time she opened it. She couldn't even remember the useless things she'd put inside. Why keep things that weren't worth remembering? She thought of climbing up the stairs, opening that door, and tossing everything in the room right out the window, but she didn't want the neighbors to see even the things she didn't care about enough keep. Strangers were the only thing keeping her from an act of complete insanity.

She felt Todd's arm slip around her waist. He stroked her ribs with one large hand, and he set his chin down on her shoulder and spoke gently into her ear. "I'm sorry."

She breathed, grateful for the contact even if she did think about pushing him down the stairs. "Sorry about what?"

"Em, I know you're lonely. I don't help things."

She patted his hand. "Sometimes you're the only thing that helps that particular thing. Don't worry about it, Todd. Normal is good." She didn't sound very reassuring, she was certain, because she was still distracted by the door at the top of the stairs. "What's in that room, Todd. Do you remember?"

"I don't know. Storage stuff I think. It doesn't matter." He took her hand in his, kissed it once, and led her up the stairs. With his hand on the small of her back, they walked past the door of nothing, up the hall of nothing, to the room they shared, which sometimes was also a room of nothing. "I'll stay with you until you fall asleep. I'm not tired, but I can sit here at least."

She gave him part of a smile and regretted at least half the time she'd spent wanting to hit him with a blunt object. By the time she pulled on her too large pajamas, pulled the band out of her tangled blond bun, and curled into the crook of his arm to fall asleep, she was convinced, at least for those few moments together, that normal was all they'd need.

3

She was most content in the back yard, and they'd paid an extra fifteen thousand dollars on the price of the house for the largest yard in the neighborhood. She needed room enough to grow things. The back yard was surrounded by an eight-foot-high cinderblock wall, and Todd had even gone so far as to fill in the gate area with cinderblocks too, completely contained. The wall was the only thing she didn't like, but she'd mostly covered it in climbers. It looked more natural than it had, but it was still a wall.

One of the primary reasons they'd chosen the house, aside from the roomy yard, was that they were one of the few communities in the city that had well water. The city water was notoriously bad and tasted like it had been sucked directly from a swimming pool, and she'd been worried that it would make her fruit taste awful.

The mornings were the best part of the day because it was her time to go into the yard and tend all those lovely, growing things. As soon as she woke up, she put on some clothes and snuck outside to her green sanctuary. Pruning and weeding wasn't exactly noisy work, but she felt the need to sneak around all the same. She wasn't nearly as tall as the wall, and there was no chance of anyone seeing her root through the dirt, but even in privacy, she never really forgot that there was a neighborhood just past the wall.

Many of the neighbors were strangers. She couldn't identify what wandering child belonged to which yard. When they'd moved in, no one had even stopped to say hello, and aside from Mr. Turlington, who came more to threaten than to welcome, she could only name a few families that lived on the street, and those only because they stood out in unpleasant ways. The Andersons were only memorable because of some domestic violence that accounted for the presence of a police car or two on the street every other week. Things had been quiet lately, and she wondered if Mr. Anderson had left his abusive wife.

Mr. Johnson was another neighborhood troublemaker. She knew him only because he was their neighbor and an odious human being. He'd had three wives at different times, but now lived alone. No one wondered how he'd ended up that way. Aside from a few drinking related noise complaints that required police intervention, Mr. Johnson was the neighborhood's resident nudist, and there was probably not a single man, woman, or child living on the block who hadn't unexpectedly gotten an eye full of Mr. Johnson's dangly bits because he never closed his curtains or wore pants. The fact that his first name was Richard, but he chose to have people call him Dick, was baffling. He wasn't exactly unfriendly, which was either a good or bad thing depending on how much old man penis she could stand to see that day.

Lately, he'd confined his bare-assery to the back yard, and he was always up early. Even as she loaded up a basket with red bell peppers, she could hear him moaning over the fence, and couldn't possibly imagine what he could be moaning about unless he was over there doing the types of inappropriate things a man who was naked all the time probably did to excess.

Today there wasn't going to be much chance of avoiding him, no matter how long she put it off. As long as she was quiet, she could usually get on with her gardening without having to play neighborly and get an eyeful, but the climbers were getting out of control and starting to spill over the tops of the wall. She was going to have to trim them, and that meant she'd be saying hello whether she wanted to or not.

It didn't yet sound like he was aware of her presence in the garden and was much too focused on moaning to himself to notice she was puttering around out there. She finished her work, opened the garden shed, and hauled the ladder to the wall which separated their yards. The moment he saw her head crest the top of the wall, Mr. Johnson groaned excitedly.

She began pruning immediately. There was no need to drag out the unpleasant pleasantries. "Good morning, Mr. Johnson, how are you?"

Mr. Johnson moaned and muttered.

"I know. It's been one of those weeks for us too." She tried not to look down, but apparently exposed parts had more gravitational pull than the sun. She glanced, and immediately regretted the lack of willpower in her eyeballs.

She managed not to grimace at his filthy blue bathrobe, untied and flapping gently in the breeze behind him. The back of it especially was badly stained, though Mr. Johnson would never admit he'd been incontinent. He was naked everywhere else.

Emily always imagined that Mr. Johnson had probably been quite good looking twenty or so years before she was born, though she never bothered to ask his age. His body seemed like it had once been muscular but had long since melted with age and miserable diet habits. His skin was a milky grey covered with a smattering of white body hair, and there was a large concentration of black veins protruding all over his body and some near his abdomen that created a sort of artistic pull to his penis, which was also covered in swollen black veins. Emily realized with a heave of revulsion that there was no earthy reason why she should be looking at Mr. Johnson's dick, again, and managed to drag her eyes up to his face and not to vomit over the fence directly onto his balding head. "I see you're getting some sun today. I think it's going to shape up to be quite nice outside."

Mr. Johnson took a shaky step toward the fence and lifted one hand toward her. She followed the direction of his fingers and saw a few black clouds on the edge of the sky. "Hopefully they will miss us, but a little rain never hurt. I know my plants will like it, and it looks like your grass wouldn't complain." Mr. Johnson's back yard was dry and unruly. She'd told him half dozen times he should install some sort of auto water irrigation system that would keep the grass green without really having to think about it, but he never did anything. Plus, that would probably require pants.

Another groan. Another shaky step. Mr. Johnson lifted his left hand where he was missing a chunk of skin on the wrist. She wasn't sure how he'd managed to take such a chunk out of himself, but she felt it would be rude to pry. The wound never seemed to heal, but it occasionally oozed a thick black blob that snaked down his hand and dripped off his fingers.

She gave him her best frown of neighborly concern. "You really should have someone look at that. It's been months. What is it about men that makes you never want to see a doctor?"

Mr. Johnson screeched, grumpy and guttural.

Emily sighed. "Well, you know best. I can't tell you what to do."

Mr. Johnson had reached the fence and craned his neck upward to stare at her. His eyes were dark green and bloodshot. She always imagined that he probably had difficulty sleeping. She wasn't certain why, except that she thought there was something wrong with him, in an emotional sense, and it seemed like people with those types of problems could never sleep. Mr. Johnson clapped his teeth at her, the skin around his lips was pulled back and very dry.

"Todd is fine, thanks for asking." She looked away, back at the garden, the green plants sprawling along the grey block wall, the dots of color nestled between the leaves, reds and oranges, and a few purple flowers she planted for no practical reason except she liked the smell of them. She was having trouble finding comfort even in the green space. "I'm sorry if we disturbed you. It seems were not very good at being married yet."

Mr. Johnson grunted and rolled his eyes back into his head a little.

She smiled. "You're right. Neither of us have tried as many times as you. Thanks. I needed a laugh today."

Mr. Johnson pressed his body against the fence and stared up at her with his eyes wide and mouth open. His tongue was dark, almost purple.

She leaned closer to him. "You want to hear a secret."

Mr. Johnson whimpered, and his purple tongue flopped excitedly between his teeth.

"Yesterday, I saw Mr. Ward sneak into Mrs. Aim's back yard, while Mrs. Ward was up the street. I think there's something going on there."

Mr. Johnson's black and white eyebrows drew together in frustration and he breathed a heavy sigh that sent a cloud of rancid breath into her face. Mr. Johnson was no better at taking care of his oral hygiene than he was at washing his bathrobe.

"I know. I shouldn't be such a busy body." Not that she felt bad about it at all. The other people on the street probably did the same thing, and she'd stop when everyone else did. She wondered what they said about her and Todd; it was probably something very cruel and not entirely inaccurate, like most gossip.

Mr. Johnson made a barking sound and pounded his oozing hand against the block wall leaving little fist curls of black ooze there.

"I don't have anything better to do." She looked away from him again, but this time, she traced the trail of a vine up the back of the house and followed the curl it made around a window.

The curtains were a pale cream color, and thick enough not to see through. She tried to think of what the room looked like on the other side, but her knees began to tremble, and the ladder wobbled. She had barely begun clipping the climbers, but the wave of dizziness was strong enough that she didn't care if they waited until tomorrow. "I should get going, Mr. Johnson. It's always nice to see you."

That was at least partially true, the part that didn't contain his body from the neck down. Mr. Johnson groaned a long, loud goodbye.

"Have a nice day."

He kept low groaning even as she put away the ladder and went inside. She had been friendly enough for one day, and the shaking of her knees had barely begun to subside.

4

Tuesday was garbage day, which made it inherently the worst day of the week. They didn't create that much garbage; she'd always preferred to compost anything that was compostable, but nonetheless, garbage happened.

There was a time before, she wasn't sure when exactly, but definitely before, when it had been Todd's job to take the garbage out, but that was when he only had to take it as far as the curb, never directly to the dump.

The dump was five miles away, which might not have felt very far if it weren't for the fact that the road had been under construction as long as she could remember, and while she did spot the occasional worker hanging around the site, she was pretty sure that no actual work had been accomplished in several months at least.

She had a theory that there was not actually a storage house for construction equipment and road cones. Instead of storing them, the city and construction companies conspired to set them up in random locations when they weren't in use, and they relied on people's unquestioning subservience to orange to keep up the ruse.

To her surprise, there were no less than three construction workers at the site, though one of them must have been a manager because he was wearing dress slacks and a tie rather than the bright orange construction vests and yellow hard hats on the other two. They weren't doing anything of course, just standing together, quavering in the sun, and staring at the ground like they might be watching slugs race, but they looked up slightly as she navigated through the loathsome orange road cones in her SUV. She waved, slathered on a smile for them, and resisted the urge to wave only with one finger instead of five since they were standing around and still not fixing the stupid road.

None of them waved back, completely rude. They were just beginning to disperse when she cleared the road cones, and she could see them take a few shoddy steps in the rear-view mirror. It looked like all of them had been drinking, which given the completely crappy state of the road after months under their care, really shouldn't have been shocking.

Mostly, the road was clear, but there were a few abandoned cars that had been rusting on the shoulder for quite some time. One little yellow VW Bug had front end damage, probably totaled, but, there were others just sitting there with the doors open, tires flat or out of gas, sometimes even with keys left in the ignition. It was unbelievable someone hadn't stolen them yet, and it was absurd that no one from the city had bothered to tow them.

Their local government was completely incompetent and had been neglecting their jobs for months. The city's failure to fulfill their basic elected duties and public services was the entire reason she had to make this irritating trip to the dump anyway. Most of the garbage trucks were sitting abandoned, some sort of worker strike, and she'd heard absolutely nothing about any effort to get them moving again.

Once she'd driven by city hall. It wasn't a place Todd told her she was allowed to go, but she's wanted to see for herself why things had gotten so bad. The place was packed with people protesting, stumbling about in the courtyard, and looking quite pathetic. It was the kind of thing she expected to see in stories of repressed foreign countries thousands of miles away, nowhere in the vicinity of her front lawn.

She slowed down as she passed one of the garbage trucks, nose in the ditch, an archaic green dinosaur dipping down for a drink on its last journey to extinction. There were bags of garbage strewn around the bed of the truck of all types, black lawn bags, green industrial bags, even the kind of little trash liners she used in the kitchen, and all the bags were duct taped together in several places and ripped in others. The back of the truck, heaped with garbage still, emanated a sweet, rotten smell that saturated the air, overwhelming even with her windows rolled all the way up.

She hit the gas and tried to out run the stench. She always did this, and it never worked. The smell followed her no matter how fast she drove. She'd heard somewhere that repeating the same action and expecting different results was the definition of insanity, but she was pretty sure that the person who thought of that had never been sandwiched between those two particular stinks before.

There was a chain-link fence around the dump, so it did nothing to contain the foulness, especially on a hot day. Emily pulled through the small gate, and the gate officer smacked a dry, bloody hand against the glass of his guardhouse as she drove through.

She wasn't exactly sure why the waste department would keep paying a guard to watch an open gate, when they couldn't figure out how to put drivers in the garbage trucks, but considering all the other local government absurdities, the guard seemed like the most innocuous mistake.

She waved, smiled in the special one hundred percent plastic way people simile when they don't give a damn. It wasn't his fault his bosses were idiots.

She backed into an open space, then covered her face with a hospital mask and a pink bandanna to try and block out some of the smell before she opened the door and circled around the SUV to get the garbage from the back. The double layer of nostril protection did not help. The smell was already in her nose and would probably be there until she went home to take a bath and gorge herself on good smelling body wash and scented candles.

She wrapped the tops of the plastic garbage bags around her hands and began walking up the path to the edge of the garbage piles. The path, lined with more black garbage bags like the ones in the back of the abandoned truck, always made her extra nauseous. They were still duct tapped in several places, and there was no reason she could think of to tape garbage bags together just to hold more garbage.

The whole place made her angry, and she clenched her fist tight around the plastic bag of her own garbage. Every now and then, she caught a quick jerk of movement from one of the bags. Walking past them felt like having several small heart attacks about every ten feet. She could only assume that rats had long since gnawed their way inside and created happy little rat homes for themselves. As she walked on, there was a breeze that hurled the rancid air and shook the plastic of the bags anywhere they were loose. It almost looked as if one of them rolled to follow her, the intruder in the land of eternal fetor and rat crap.

She quickened her pace; the soles of her shoes thumping, sometimes squishing on the dirt, until she reached a reasonable place to throw her bags. She pitched them to the top of the pile; the bag clattered and rolled down a little but settled without blocking the path, and the job was done. Then all she wanted to do was to race her gag reflex home and see which of them made it first.

If it wasn't for the distinct sound of something crunching a little further up the path, she would have jogged back to the car and sped all the way home, road cones be damned, but an argument broke out between rational judgement, her primal instinct, and morbid curiosity. Even if she could figure out what the sound was, she probably didn't want to know. There was no reasonable outcome that ended well in her current location, and her eyes were beginning to burn and water from the grossness. She could practically see the stink rising around her, but curiosity was victorious. She held her breath and rounded a trash pile, her hand instinctively slipping around the handle of the small gun she'd slipped into her front pocket for the ride.

It was a dog. She was both relieved and surprised. It was laying on its stomach next to one of the duct taped garbage bags, which it had shredded open to get breakfast. Part of the rancid meat was still in the bag, but the dog chewed contentedly on the bone, breaking it apart a little at a time with its teeth.

It had the kind of ears that flopped down to either side of its head, and its fur was a pretty shade of yellow, except in some places where it was matted with red and black.

It noticed her but didn't stop chewing until she tried to call for it. She deliberated about this for some time while trying not to puke. It looked like the kind of dog that might want to cuddle, but also might want to eat her face off. She decided she wasn't willing to yell and risk startling the dog and instead, clicked her tongue against her cheek. The dog acknowledged her by looking up from its bone and tilting its head slightly.

She slipped off the small backpack Todd made her carry everywhere, unzipped it searching for some kind of dog appropriate lure, and found an old bag still half full of unfinished jerky. There wasn't much of it left, but she stuck her hand toward the dog in what she hoped looked like a friendly offering. The dog got up immediately and trotted over; its nimble paws far better suited to climbing garbage heaps than Emily's sneakers. The dog swallowed the jerky in almost one bite, and she let it finish the rest of the bag before sticking out her empty hand again in a different kind of offering. The dog shoved its large head into her hand and allowed her to scratch it behind its floppy ears. Its fur felt a little sticky and gross, like it hadn't had a bath and had been rolling in garbage for quite a while.

"Hi. . ." She looked beneath the dog for the required dog gender check ". . .boy. Hi baby. You all alone?"

She rolled her eyes at herself. It sounded like she was trying to pick up a date in a bar almost as much as trying to talk to a dog in the dump.

The dog wore a pale blue collar that had faded with the sun and frayed badly at the edges, but there were no tags attached to the collar that could have helped her identify the owner. From the state of its fur, she guessed it had been loose quite some time. She couldn't remember seeing fliers anywhere for a missing dog. From his eagerness, she figured he had been lonely quite some time too. Even as strangers they had that much in common aside from smelling like a portable toilet housed in deepest level of hell.

The dog lifted its head and sniffed the air, then growled like he had decided to rip her face off after all. She felt his fur stand up under her fingers before holding up hands in what she hoped translated to surrender. "I'm sorry!"

The dog looked at her in clear exasperation as he climbed a little up the heap where he waited, staring back at her, and then staring into the dump, and then staring at her, and then staring at the dump, and finally walking back down the pile to her, then back up the pile while looking at her.

When she realized she was supposed to follow, she felt like an idiot. "I'm sorry." She whispered cautiously. "I don't speak dog." Emily climbed up on hands and knees to crouch behind the dog, sinking into the heap. She felt her jeans soaking with something wet and smelly, but she scanned the dump beside the panting dog, trying to follow its nervous gaze. At first, she saw nothing, and she reached up to tell the dog so by rubbing the back of his neck. His fur was still at attention, so she looked again.

This time she saw it, something moving, far away, at least half the length of the dump. "It's just someone else dropping off the garbage."

The dog was unrelenting. The longer she watched, the clearer it was why the dog had such interest. She watched as whatever it was climbed a garbage heap with all the agility of the dog, only on two legs. It grabbed a bag and tossed it down the garbage hill. Too much coordination, it, he, she guessed from his height, was like her, human. She sighed at the stupidity of her own thought. Everyone was human, but this guy. . .

She allowed herself to sink lower into the garbage pile, and watched the man moving through the dump. He was very tall, with spindly legs that made him look like a clothed spider and had black hair.

There was a moment when she was excited to tell Todd something as interesting as seeing a man throwing garbage, right up till the moment she thought that Todd might never let her leave the house again. There only so many places she could go and even a trip to the dump was something other than the walls of their house. Worse, he might think she was getting sick again. Todd was never going to believe her; this strange man was an impossible thing. He was Bigfoot, or Chupacabra. He was the Loch Ness Monster of the city dump.

And monsters, even impossible ones, were terrifying. She backed slowly down the garbage pile, careful not to make any sound that might draw the stranger's attention. The minute her sneakers hit the dirt she barreled for the SUV, the dog sprinting beside her. She dashed past the terrible black, wriggling bags and onto the pavement, threw open the driver's side door, and skid to an unplanned halt. In the split second the door was open, the dog had leapt past her into the passenger seat, getting everything on him all over the upholstery.

"No, Dog." She hissed. "Get down."

The dog must have misheard; or she was still very bad at talking to dogs. He sat down instead and stared at her with his eyebrows raised. Emily looked back over her shoulder in the direction of the stranger. She couldn't see him anymore; she doubted he'd even noticed her. There probably wasn't any immediate danger.

She could go around to the passenger door, put the dog out onto the pavement, and head home. But the entire time she was considering she had enough time to do that, she was also thinking that the dog was pretty cute, and she was lonely, and he was lonely, and just as afraid of that strange man as she was. "Fine." She grumbled quietly. "But Todd isn't going to like it."

Despite an overwhelming gagging feeling and a pounding heart from the jaunt back to the car, Emily grinned at the face she imagined Todd would make when he walked in that evening. "Good. Good dog."

The dog stared impatiently out the front window. She climbed in, slammed the door, and pulled from the parking lot. The guard at the gate waved again, but she was scratching the dog's ears and didn't bother to wave back.

5

"Good boy." Emily cooed at the dog. She'd had to carry him through the house. The carpets were light and both of them were filthy, but her shoes weren't quite as dire as the state of the dog's paws. He was large, and she was not exactly a professional heavy doggy lifter. He also didn't take well to the idea of being carried and squirmed so much going up the stairs she was sure they were both going to end up back at the bottom again in a pile.

Once she got him in the tub, he seemed to recognize bath time as something familiar, harmless, and necessary. He stood quite still in the water and let Emily cover him in shampoo. She didn't have any dog shampoo, so she used her own. At least he would have ultra-hydration and body control.

After the third douse of shampoo and all over scrubbing, it was clear that whatever grossness he'd run through at the dump was never going to be entirely clean. Parts of his yellow fur would be permanently stained red and black, particularly around his mouth, which was more difficult to wash. "I'm sorry boy. I tried. I think you're just going to have to stay red."

The dog looked up at her, dripped, panted happily, and smelled like it had just gotten back from a long vacation in Hawaii.

"I'll call you Red." She rubbed his wet head behind the ears with one hand while she drained the horrible grey bath water. He seemed to enjoy the rub down with a fluffy green towel and didn't bother to do the stereotypical full body boogie she'd been expecting. "Red." She said firmly. The dog looked at her with what she could only assume was some measure of approval.

She had about two hours until Todd got home, and she spent part of the time waiting showing Red around. She took him out to the garden. He loved it as much as she did. He darted back and forth on the grass like someone had lit his tail on fire, and it took a while for him to slow down enough for her to show him a place beside the house where he could use the bathroom. She was glad they had another thing in common and promised she would make Todd build him a doggy door, so he could come in and out as he pleased as long as he didn't bark or growl at Mr. Johnson. She also whispered to him that Mr. Johnson was always naked, but that was mainly conversational since Red would never be expected to peer over the fence.

She also took him inside and showed him the sofa, and which place was Todd's so Red could be sure to lay in Todd's spot as often as possible. After Red gave her a hopeful look, she encouraged him to jump up on the couch and sat down beside him. It took a few minutes for his guilt to wear off, and she suspected he'd never been allowed on furniture before. After a few tight circles, he finally laid down, flopped his still damp head in her lap, and was content to lay there and be petted.

The contentment she felt from this snuggle time was potent. She felt lighter, or was that happiness? Maybe feeling happy was enough to make her think she was happy, and she stayed that way for a full hour until she had to get up and start making dinner.

Dogs apparently were not the cure for crappy, irritable cooking, whatever other problems he might solve. Red didn't follow her into the kitchen, and she thought he must have been tired from being outside alone for so long because he fell into such a deep sleep she could hear him snoring in the other room.

She watched the clock, which was shaped like a cow, because everything in the kitchen was cow. She had cow salt and pepper shakers, cow hot plates, cow dishrags and wash cloths, a cow cookie jar, about fifty little useless little porcelain cows sitting on the back of the counter, one that dispensed toothpicks from the udders, and one that dispensed brown, root beer flavored jelly beans out its butt when she tugged on its tail. There was also a cow piggy bank, which she'd mainly purchased for the irony.

Todd was as punctual as ever and came into the kitchen to kiss her on the forehead. She smiled and said nothing but hello. That should have been his first clue that something weird was about to occur. She never just smiled and said hello without wanting to whap him with a wooden spoon. Todd was oblivious and walked into the other room as he always did.

She was stifling giggles with her hands even before Todd shouted at her. "What the hell is this?"

"It's a dog, Todd." She called back fighting to keep the laughter out of her voice and smiling so hard it hurt her cheeks.

"I know it's a dog." He shouted, a cannon of annoyance. "What's it doing in the house?"

She put a hand over her mouth again and composed herself before she shut off the stove and went to stand in the doorway between the living room and the kitchen. "Resting."

"No." Todd said in a tone so fatherly it aged him forty years. She could practically see his nose hairs turning grey. "We aren't keeping it."

"No." She said with equal firmness. "We aren't. I am. It's my dog, his name is Red, and you will get over it, dear."

He blinked at her for a moment at first

surprised at her insistence, then awash with confusion as he glanced over his shoulder at the dog. "But it's yellow."

"Yeah. Most of him. Anyway, he matches the formal room, so obviously I have to keep him."

Todd was so dumbfounded his eyes were partially crossed. "But it's yellow;" he annunciated the last word at her as if he might be ready to spell it for her also.

"It's my dog. I'll call him what I want. He likes it."

"How do you know what he likes?"

She huffed in exasperation. "Here, Red." Red almost instantly bounded into the Kitchen with his tail wagging. "Red, this is Todd. Todd meet Red."

To their mutual surprise, Red held up a paw for him to shake. She could only smile, as Todd bent down to accept the offered paw with all the awkwardness of a man who didn't want to be incredibly rude. The paw turned out to be little more than a carefully planned ploy to get Todd to bend down. As soon as it was in range, Red licked Todd's face.

Todd drew back looking slightly like the Hulk, in that his face had turned green and he gagged so hard that the veins stuck out in his neck. "Christ. What the hell has it been eating?"

"Don't say 'it' like he's some kind of monster. He is a he. I found him at the dump. I would assume he's been eating rotten meat and garbage. It'll probably clear up eventually."

Todd looked in imminent danger of puking on the kitchen floor. It felt like the right time to tell him dinner was ready. She handed Todd one of the three plates she prepared, and then set another on the floor for Red, who ate with a frenzy.

"You're letting him eat off our plates?"

"Well yeah. What else would I do? I can't just throw it on the floor."

Todd slathered on his best fatherly simper, a mixture of scolding and sweet. "Em, we can't keep it. We can't afford the extra mouth to feed, especially if you're going to feed him what we eat."

"The human food is only temporary, until I get some proper dog food. Besides, we throw away more than enough to feed him, and most of that is what I don't eat."

He looked like he wanted to do more scolding, or screaming, she wasn't sure which. In the end, Todd just looked down at his plate. "What is this anyway?"

She chewed her lip uncomfortably. "Uhm. Chicken."

Todd raised an eyebrow. "It looks like pork again."

"I'll say its pork if that's what you'd rather eat." She realized it wasn't a complaint exactly, but she really wished Todd would just eat and not make her tell him what it was every day. It was such a strange necessity, that information, like he expected her to poison him or secretly serve him her own finger.

"Whatever." Todd turned back into the living room and spoke over his shoulder as if it would be the last word on the subject. "We're not keeping the dog."

Em grabbed her own plate, resisted the urge to chuck it at the back of Todd's head like a ceramic Frisbee, and followed him into the living room. "You don't get to decide that. You don't just get to make decisions for me."

"You didn't even ask me first. You don't seem to mind making decisions without me. Shouldn't it work both ways?"

"Sure, but other than having to share the sofa, this decision doesn't affect you, and it makes a big difference to me."

"What made you just suddenly adopt a dirty dog?"

"He's not dirty. I washed him three times. He smells like coconuts."

"Tell that to his breath."

"I didn't think about it. I didn't have time. We were running away from a man we saw. Red just jumped in the car, and I drove off. But he's a good boy and he deserves a nice place to live as much as anybody. I'd have taken him home if he'd been wearing a tag, but he just had an old collar on and nothing else."

"Em, we don't need a dog." Todd was almost to the point of yelling at her, but in a moment of silence, his face began to shift from stubbornness to something more like concern. His eyebrows drew together thoughtfully, and he grew quieter again. "What man at the dump?"

"I don't know. I didn't stop to talk to him."

"Did he come after you?"

"He was far away. I doubt he saw me."

Todd pinched the center of his nose. "Are you sure it wasn't the gate guard?"

"Of course. He waved to me on the way in like he always does. This was someone different. I mean really different."

"You saw someone? I mean human."

"They're all human, Todd."

"Damnit, Em. You know what I mean." His eyes flashed with real anger and his voice deepened to a tone that was all fear and commanding.

"Yeah. I did." She knew he wouldn't believe her, but his reaction to this information was darker than she expected. She regretted telling him at all. She wished they had the kind of relationship where she could tell him things and he wouldn't accuse her of being crazy, but that wasn't the way of it.

Todd's voice had returned to disbelief, and his eyes aloof, scathing. "That's impossible."

Em shoved a hunk of potato into her mouth that she picked off her plate with two fingers. "I thought it was impossible too, but he was throwing garbage bags around like he was looking for something. Most people don't do that when I see them in the dump."

"What did he look like?" Todd seemed like he was saying something that was quite different than the something he wanted to say. Lines formed on his forehead with the effort of restraint.

She half wished he'd scream at her. Sometimes his patience, his self-control was the worst thing. It made him cold. How could someone be both cold and loving? That was the real impossibility. "He was tall and had black hair. He was far off; I couldn't really see his face or anything. He had legs like a spider."

Todd seemed to calm even further. He released the bridge of his nose and returned to fathering her like she was some over imaginative child. "Em, honey. You know you didn't really see anything."

Emily set her plate down on the edge of the sofa knowing good and well that Red was going to have at it before she could finish, but her stomach was in knots anyway and there was no point in forcing food into it. Red immediately went for the plate, and in his excitement of licking the thing, knocked it into the floor where it shattered on the carpet. Emily jumped slightly at the sound but didn't bend down to pick up the pieces. "I'm not crazy, Todd. I know what I saw."

"I believe you thought you saw someone, but you couldn't have seen that, honey. It could only have been, I mean, it couldn't have been a real person."

Emily crossed her arms over her chest and tried to quell tremors of frustration in her arms. If he were going to be cold, then she also would try to be. "What the hell does that even mean? All people are real people. It's not like there's some factory out there cranking out fake humans and sending them out in the world to confuse me. I wouldn't even have seen him if it weren't for Red. Red saw him first, so I know he was there." Logical enough, she believed, even for Todd's strict sense of information processing. He couldn't dispute the validity of two pairs of eyes.

He didn't even try. "Babe, I get that you're lonely, and maybe we can talk about getting a dog that hasn't been living in a dump, but you're obviously having deeper issues if you've started hallucinating."

He was barely even listening, so convinced that she was crazy that no amount of evidence would convince him otherwise. She felt fire rise to her eyes. "Yeah, I'm having issues, and they are all you. I wasn't hallucinating. I saw him. Why do you treat me like I'm insane?"

"I don't treat you like you're insane." Todd rolled his eyes.

This only exacerbated her annoyance and illustrated her point. "You think I'm insane about you treating me like I'm insane."

"Because you didn't see anyone!" Todd was yelling now. She couldn't understand why he'd be so enraged. It didn't matter to them if she saw something or she didn't. If she did see someone, that person was far away and didn't know where they lived. If she didn't, which she was sure was not the case, it didn't matter because it wasn't real. His evident outrage most likely did not have the effect he intended.

It only made her feel colder, sullen. "Tomorrow use that machine at work to make Red a new tag and bring home the stuff to put in a doggy door."

"You are not keeping the damn dog!"

"Then you are not keeping your damn wife." It wasn't even a threat. There was nothing in her but flatness. "Do what I said, Todd. Or I swear to God, I'll build you a house in the yard."

Todd snorted and rubbed his forehead; his face was quite red, but he'd returned to his condescending parent voice again. "You don't want me to think you're insane, but you're acting like a maniac."

"I doesn't matter if I act normal, or crazy, or cold. You'll keep treating me the same way. You don't change, even if I do."

"Because you always act like you've lost your mind." He was beginning to pout.

The fact that he was attempting to sway her sympathies only pissed her off more. "You think so? Just wait. I have not yet begun to show you crazy. I'm keeping the dog. It's not a request. It's not a conversation. It's not even something that's about to happen, it has already. You can get the hell over it, and next time the garbage starts piling up you can take it to the dump yourself, like before. I hate that place."

Todd's face went pale; his voice hollowed and dropped to almost nothing. "What do you mean, like before?"

She could almost think he'd been more afraid than angry just then. She couldn't blame him for feeling afraid. She'd seen it with her own eyes and run like hell. Even the dog had been afraid. She felt her emotions ebbing back to calmness. "You used to take the garbage out, when the trucks still came, you took it to the curb."

"You remember the trucks coming?"

She felt confused enough to procced with caution. She wished she'd grabbed a couple of the orange road cones to help her navigate her marriage. "It wasn't that long ago."

"Why would you suddenly think about that?"

"I don't know. But you did it before, and you can do it again. I won't."

"Okay."

"I'm serious, Todd."

"I said okay."

6

That night Todd slept downstairs. Emily thought he didn't really mean to; it didn't feel like he'd deliberately avoided their bed. He fell asleep on the sofa while he watched movies, and she curled up with Red in silence like stone. She thought maybe, as she and Red headed up to bed, that he would wake up in the night and come up stairs to join them, but when she woke up in the morning, with sweaty feet because Red was sleeping on them, Todd had left them alone all night and had already left for work.

Sleep was enough to cool her temper and kindle her regret. Though she had no intention of giving up her new furry friend, because she was already completely in love with Red, she still felt bad about the way she'd brought him up to Todd. She had only wanted to surprise him, to knock him off his guard, but sometimes she was a real bitch and didn't realize it till long after the fact. Sometimes she even felt bad about it. Red lifted his head and stared at her sleepily.

"I did a bad thing, Red." Red wiggled up the bed, crawling on his stomach to lay his head on her chest. "I need to fix it." The heat of the dog radiating through her was comforting, but she laid there feeling like a crappy person for another ten minutes before she had absorbed enough snuggles to motivate herself. She pushed the dog gently off, so she could climb out of bed. "Breakfast first."

To the idea of food, Red heartily agreed; he leapt off the bed and squirmed by the door impatiently waiting for her to throw on a robe and follow him downstairs. She heated up some water for a cup of cocoa even though it was too warm for it, then threw a slab of meat for Red in the microwave to take the chill off. She didn't bother with the plate and dropped it directly on the floor. She was pretty sure he'd clean up his own mess, and Red had swallowed all of the meat and was lapping at the tile before she peeled her apple.

His back half was cleaning the tile, his tail wagging as she rooted through the cabinets. It had been a while since she decided she needed to make some kind of offering of apology, and the last thing she wanted to do first thing in the morning was any kind of cooking, but she decided after a few minutes to make Todd some snickerdoodles. They were his favorite, but she almost never made them due to cooking related homicidal rage. It had been so long, she couldn't even remember the last time. She couldn't remember Todd ever telling her that his favorite cookie was a snickerdoodle, but she felt confident in the information even though it floated seemingly unconnected to anything else.

Before she did the awful deed of crafting apologetic cookies, she cleaned up the broken plate in the living room, then went outside to the garden to pluck weeds and soak up a bit of sunlight. She needed all the emotional fortitude she could get, not just for cooking, but for the task of apologizing. She was able to stay incredibly silent while she worked, and aside from a few sad cries, Mr. Johnson left her alone, even with Red dashing around like an idiot.

When she finally did come back inside, it took less than an hour to finish the cookies. They turned out well, which was a complete surprise, and she managed to get through baking without breaking, burning, or throwing anything. She put the warm cookies in a plastic container and packed them in her backpack. She also packed the other necessities of travel, snacks for both human and dog, extra ammo. When she was ready to leave she went rooting through the garage where she found some thin rope that would work as a leash. Red let her tie it to his collar, but she stood there looking at the rope and felt bad for tying him after he'd lately been used to roaming so free. She had the feeling that she probably didn't have to leash him at all, that he wanted her around as much as she wanted him, which was a lovely feeling, even if the only person who wanted her around was a dog. She untied the rope and Red sat down at her feet.

There was no smart reason to walk. The neighborhood, despite the upper middle-class veneer, had been especially dangerous lately; still she had the opposite problem from Red, she spent too much time tied up, and needed a little while of breezes and exercise. She did not count going to the dump as either breezes or exercise, except for the running away. Red was not remotely tired from his laps around the yard and made it very clear when she opened the front door that he would enjoy a bit more room to burn off his indefatigable energy.

The plan was to walk to Todd's workplace, which wasn't particularly far away, so she reasoned that between the dog and herself, they could keep each other safe. Todd worked at a local hardware store that was only about a mile and a half from their house. He'd taken the job at a pay cut because the previous company he worked for installing solar panels had gone under. The frustrating thing, he told her, was not that the company had failed, but that it had only failed because its CEO was defrauding the company into bankruptcy. He felt like his, and all the other employees' hard work had gone to waste. Todd missed working outside, but he didn't seem to hate the hardware store either. He'd gotten a promotion to manager, though she couldn't recall how long ago that had been, and he was a tough boss.

A little under an hour later when she and Red strolled into the door of the hardware store, she said hello to the cashier who was zip tied to the counter next to the register. He was a tall, balding man with a big pot belly that made him look older than he probably was. He'd probably taken too many smoke breaks and was longing for another cigarette, because he groaned with frustration as she and Red went by. She felt a little sorry for him. The zip tie was cutting into his wrist and a small glob of black had formed around the tie. She gave him a smile, hoping to cheer him up a bit, but he only groaned again and chewed the air as though it were made of nicotine.

It took a while to find Todd. She walked across practically the whole store and all she found were more zip-tied employees and a customer wandering through the appliances. She and Red slipped down an adjacent aisle to give the customer some space, because the customer looked like she had questions about refrigerators and Emily didn't want to be called on for an opinion. The customer was banging a fist against a refrigerator door hard enough to hear at some distance, and Emily could hardly blame her for her irritation, since there weren't any employees in this part of the store at all. It was always that way though, there was never someone around when they were needed, and fifteen employees crowding an aisle when they were just stocking shelves and getting in the way.

She found Todd in the manager's office, leaning back in his computer chair with his hands behind his head, staring at the ceiling light. She watched him for a minute to see if he'd notice her, but Todd sometimes had the situational awareness of a sloth. She finally had to get his attention, because she couldn't determine if he was sleeping with his eyes open. "Todd?" She said from the door. "What are you doing?"

He sat up so quickly he almost slid out of the chair, and he sputtered out his answer. "I'm on break." His surprise wore off quickly. He frowned, first her, then even more so at the dog. "What are you doing here?"

"We wanted to come and see you." Emily scratched Red's ears to comfort him, but it was a useless gesture. The dog didn't seem perturbed.

Todd's frown deepened. He leaned forward in the chair, propped his elbows up on the desk, and crossed his arms. "You can't just show up at my job like this. I'm on the clock."

He sounded completely fatherly again. She'd never thought about it, but she wondered if he used that same voice to his zip tied employees to keep them in their sections. 'Now Frank, I think you've had one too many smoke breaks today. Give me your hands so I can zip you to the counter. You know this is for the best.'

She sighed but tried to sound chipper. It wouldn't do to pick a fight when she was there to apologize, even if he was making her want to apologize less by the minute. "I thought you said you were on break." She took off her backpack and put it on his desk. "We brought you something."

He looked at the dog, his nose scrunched in skepticism. "We?"

It was impossible to keep the eye roll from her voice, even if she managed to keep her eyes still in her head. "Obviously, me and Red."

"So?" Todd blinked at her as if she was going to spring some other terrible surprise on him at any second, like maybe she found a few cats and squirrel she also intended to keep.

"I made snickerdoodles." She pulled the plastic container from her backpack and thrust it toward him. "You said they were your favorite, didn't you?"

She thought he'd be pleased, maybe even happy, but Todd looked as though someone had let his air out and he slumped in his chair like a flat tire. "I didn't know you remembered that."

She didn't understand why he wasn't even a little grateful. She thought maybe she had remembered incorrectly, and he was actually deathly allergic to snickerdoodles or they gave him diarrhea or something. "But I'm right, aren't I?"

"Yeah." He took the box of cookies and peeled off the plastic lid. He didn't take one, but he stared at them in the container as if they were some kind of oddity which might jump out of the box, attach themselves to his face, and proceed to suck out his brain. "Thanks."

She was starting to feel sad, which masqueraded as frustrated. Why couldn't cookies just fix everything? "I wanted to say sorry. I know I've been weird."

Todd stopped studying the snickerdoodles to examine her instead. "It's fine," he said, but she felt like he was still expecting some sort of malicious end game.

"No, it isn't. I shouldn't just crap on you every time there's something wrong with me." She put the brakes on just in time to keep from adding, 'now eat your fucking cookies.'

"Really." Todd stared back at the cookies, trying to avoid looking at her. "It's fine."

"Okay." She said, though not really feeling as much ease to her conscience as she had hoped, and much more annoyance than she'd anticipated. "I guess Red and I should go. By the way, you've got a customer waiting in appliances. They seem pretty annoyed already, might help if they see a manager."

Todd nodded and grabbed a long-handled axe that was leaning against the drawers of his desk. "I'll go take care of them."

"Okay. Enjoy the cookies." Emily gave him half a smile and prepared to go, but Todd reached out and got hold of her arm. "Wait a minute." He paused as though he were considering what to say. "I don't want that customer to think I've been in here slacking off. They'll just get angrier."

"Yeah, okay."

"Let me go help the customer, and then I'll turn on the tag machine for you, and you can make Red whichever one you want."

Emily felt like the insides of her chest were suddenly larger than her rib cage could manage. "Really, Todd?"

He squeezed her arm. "Yeah, just stay here okay? Shut the door behind me."

He left with his axe, and she shut the door. Red laid down on the floor. Emily sat down on Todd's desk to wait for him and stole a cookie to share with Red, who seemed unhappy with the cinnamon but ate his half anyway. Todd came back in less than five minutes. His shirt was badly stained.

"All done?" She pointed to the stains on his shirt. "What happened?"

"Nothing interesting. I hate it when people just come in to bitch with no intention of buying anything." Todd laid the axe down and a black pool formed beneath it on the floor. "They're gone now. Come with me."

He reached out a hand for her to take,

which she looked at with about the same skepticism as he had the cookies. She couldn't remember the last time they'd held hands, even for a few minutes. She slid her fingers inside his and remembered with no small degree of delight how much larger his hands were than hers, and the feeling of her hand disappearing in the heat of his. He led her to the front of the store where the tag machine was set up. It wasn't an easy task to plug it in; the wall socket was behind the machine, and Todd struggled to move it out far enough to slide his hand behind it. He explained that people didn't ask for it very often, so there was no reason to keep it going. She thought it was probably easier to keep it going than to have to move a small mountain every time someone wanted a three-dollar dog tag but didn't say anything.

She picked out a red tag shaped like a bone, and they watched in silence as the machine engraved Red's name and address on the tag. When it was done, it dropped into a tray, and Todd fished it out with two fingers. "Here."

"Thanks." She took the tag and attached it to Red's collar while he sat panting. The tag looked good, but he was going to need a new collar soon. She didn't think it was the time to bring that up. She'd already had one bit of progress and didn't want to push her luck. "It looks really good."

Todd looked at the dog with indifference.

For a while, all they had to listen to was the disgruntled moaning of Todd's zip tied employee. The silence went on so long she started to feel uncomfortable. "Todd?"

He sighed and stared at the concrete. "I'm sorry too, Em. I mean, if you feel like you want to take my head off, it's probably my fault."

Emily laughed a little, which, given the source of her amusement, was a rare and marvelous thing. "It's like you read my mind."

The cashier grunted and pulled against the zip tie, waiving his loose arm frantically.

Todd glared at the cashier, but his face was gentler when he spoke to her. "I should get back to work but thank you for the cookies. I'm sorry I've been a jerk. Let me try to make it up to you?"

She lifted an eyebrow. "What do you have in mind?"

"I don't know. It's been a while since we went out somewhere together. Didn't you say you wanted some new clothes?"

Emily stared at him with so much skepticism she thought he might suffer spontaneous combustion. "You want to take me shopping?"

"Yeah. I mean, I don't want to. I hate shopping, but you hate baking, so that's kind of the point, if that's what you want..."

"Shopping is good." She rushed to get the words out before he changed his mind.

"I'll see if I can get tomorrow off, okay?"

"Is there someone to cover you?" From the grim faces she'd seen on the cashier and the other employees, she didn't think any of them would be willing to do him a favor.

"I'll work it out," he kissed her forehead, "for you."

"Thanks, Todd."

"I better get back." Todd looked over his shoulder at the cashier again.

"I understand. I'll see you at home." Em kissed Todd on the cheek and waved goodbye to the cashier, who barely lifted an arm in response.

The first steps she took were toward home, but Emily felt better. It was a lovely day. It may have also been a lovely day because she felt better. The sky was mostly cloudless, and it was blue and breezy. Red was still bounding with energy, and it seemed a shame to go home to the confines of the house when it was so delectably fine out.

She decided without a full second's deliberation to take the long way home. When it was time to take the shortcut through an unfinished portion of the subdivision where the block walls had not yet been built, she walked past to circle around the block. Red wove around her, sniffed the grass, and peed on half the neighborhood.

The subdivision where they'd bought the house was part of a large master planned community. All of the houses were basically just copies of each other from the outside but scattered far enough apart from their clones that it seemed less factory generated. All the lawns had rules about the number and type of plants each person had to maintain, rules about where to park the cars, rules about keeping garbage cans off the street, even rules about drilling for oil and starting mining operations, because apparently if those things weren't expressly forbidden, some person would undoubtedly decide that a subdivision geared for families was the perfect place to drop an oil rig or drill for diamonds. There were parks and greenbelts scattered throughout which put additional space between houses, made the neighborhood attractive, and provided a romping place for unsupervised children. Red particularly enjoyed the greenbelts. Every time he came to one, he would dash across it and back several times until he wheezed with exhaustion, but by the next green place, he was always ready again.

She liked watching him play. There was something free in a wagging tail she thought she'd probably never feel except vicariously. Even in the dump, he hadn't seemed unhappy, even if he'd been in a hurry to adopt her as his own. It would be nice if people treated each other the way they treated good dogs. She wished that Todd would open the front door and call for her; she'd be so happy to see him that she'd barrel through the house and jump up on him, so he could rub and kiss her and tell her she was a good human. Even though things were better for the moment, she doubted Todd would ever be that eager to see her, and even more so doubted that she would ever be happy enough to wag her tail for him.

The longer she walked, the more she had time to think, the worse she felt. She found herself wanting to be shut up again, regretting everything she'd done that day including apologizing. They were a few blocks from home when they spotted another grassy area nestled between houses. Red trotted ahead in anticipation of another insane doggy dash, but he didn't sprint as usual.

She slowed as he slowed. He stopped at the edge of the house that bordered the park and growled. He got a Mohawk between his shoulder blades when he growled, like a K-9 early warning system for danger, and she knew something was wrong. She pulled the gun from her hip holster and walked slowly up to where red was sounding the alert. Even before she could see around the fence, she heard the squeal of metal on metal. "Red, quiet."

Red managed to lower the volume of his growl at almost the same moment that she saw what he was so upset about. There was a little boy tangled in a rusty swing. On one side, the chain had broken, and he'd gotten caught up in it like some snared wild animal in the jungle. He couldn't have been more than four or five, and he hissed and kicked his little feet without being able to reach the ground. He was wearing a red shirt, and the chain was wrapped several times around his chest and arms, but she could see the emblem of a superhero printed there.

Now he flew like his hero, and she thought that should make her happy, that the little boy was playing and had learned to fly. Happiness was fluid and she was full of holes. The little boy's face was nearly black with veins; one of his shoes was gone, and one of his socks was soaked with red and black beneath a hunk of him that was missing from his upper leg. They were full of holes together.

"Hello." She sounded so sad that she was worried she would frighten him. She tried to pull her voice up, even if her heart felt like a sack of bricks clunking in her chest. "Are you alone?"

He snarled, his voice high pitched and innocent. She took a step toward the boy, but Red scooted in front her like a yellow roadblock. "We have to get him down Red. He can't stay that way."

The little boy twisted his head so far to one side she thought his neck might break.

"Where's your mother?"

He kicked so hard he rattled the remaining chain, and the motion caused him to oscillate back and forth. With the swaying; he became a blur and watching him swing was so hypnotic she became a blur as well. She heard kids laughing and someone calling her name. She blinked and shapeless faces whirled by; she wondered if she knew them.

She wanted to know where her mother was, and she began to doubt that she'd ever really been a child. There was so much she'd forgotten. If she'd had a mother, she couldn't remember the woman's face. Grey hair? Short, hunched shoulders from working. Aged hands washing dishes in the sink. She could almost feel her mother's hands, squeezing her shoulders and pulling her away from the little boy writhing in the chains.

Red roared like he was made more of bear than dog; Emily felt cold. Why were her mother's hands so cold? Fingers dug into her shoulders, and the pain made everything come into focus again.

She twisted, trying to heave the cold hands away. The mother was much too strong, and had her hands twisted into Emily's shirt. Emily drove an elbow backward into the woman who had come to claim her son, but the blow did very little to aid escaping. She didn't have time to think about anything but gnashing teeth as she struggled, but she saw Red, a yellow lightning bolt, fly up and into the fray. The force of him knocked the mother and Emily both to the ground, but the mother lost her grip as they fell, and Emily was free.

Emily rolled across the tall grass and lifted up to see the face of the woman who'd left her son alone. The woman had the same eyes, the same childlike mouth as the boy in the swing. Emily had dropped the gun when she'd hit the ground, and her eyes darted between it and the woman who crawled closer. She thought about diving for the gun, but Red was faster than she could ever be. Red sank his teeth into the back of the woman's neck. She opened her mouth in fury and pain, but with a few vicious jerks of Red's teeth, she was still.

Slowly, Emily climbed to her feet. She walked with caution to her weapon and picked it up with one hand; with the other, she wiped away the memory that had almost made her forget herself by dusting the grass off her jeans. She gripped the gun and leveled it at the back of the woman's head, pulled the trigger, and watched broken skull scatter across the grass.

The boy in the swing wailed, and the mournfulness of his voice made her chest feel like she'd been shot herself. Emily sat down and pulled her knees to her chest. "I'm sorry," she rubbed her eyes with the back of one wrist. The boy screamed so loud he couldn't have heard her apologize again. "So sorry."

Red came to Emily, hovering by her side,

his fur still spiked like he was ready to join a punk band. She stroked his shoulders, and after a minute or two, she felt him begin to relax. "You were a good boy. You saved me even when I couldn't see."

Red stared at the little boy, frenzied on his chain leash; Emily followed his gaze to the boy's wild face. "We can't leave him now that his mother is gone."

Red sat down in the grass beside her, and looked over his shoulder, down the road that would take them home. "He's too small to be on his own." She stood up with a small groan. Her shoulders ached where the mother had gotten hold. Emily's shoes were speckled with black, and Red would certainly need another bath.

She walked over to the boy thrashing in the chains and reached above him to grip the chain at the boy's back and hold him somewhat still. "It's okay, baby." She took aim again, but her hand was shaking; she took a breath and looked away. She couldn't do it, not that way. Emily took off her backpack and got a knife. It seemed gentler, somehow more humane, even as the bright sun danced along the blade. She went back to the boy, held the chain again, and brought the blade down into the base of his skull.

To her horror, the boy still squirmed and wailed. She'd only injured him and made him more afraid. She was too weak inside to be strong for him, and she had to pull the knife out and try again to get it in his brain. This time she blinked away tears as she watched the knifepoint slide into the boy and felt the thump of the knife hilt as it hit the boy's skull. He went limp and wasn't crying or flying anymore. Carefully, she untangled him from the mess of chains and swing. He weighed almost nothing as she laid him down beside his mother.

"See? It's better this way."

Red leaned against her leg.

"We did the right thing." Even as she said the words, it didn't feel right. She looked up at the sky, which was cloudier than she remembered, and shivered in the breeze that chilled her much more than it had only minutes before. She couldn't stand to stay in the park another second, or she thought she might lay down next to the boy and his mother and never get up again.

She rushed home, practically at a run, Red a few paces behind her. She didn't even bother to wave to the neighbors as she passed. It was like there were no neighbors at all, and she and Todd were the only people in the world. At home, she locked the door behind Red and he went directly upstairs to the bathroom, as eager to be clean of what had happened as Emily. She climbed into the tub with Red and tried to wash away everything they'd seen.

When they had exhausted the hot water,

Emily shut off the shower and grabbed towels for them both, wrapping her hair in one, and Red in the other. "It's better if we don't tell Todd," She said, squatting down to rub him with the towel. "We've only just made things okay with him."

When Todd got home that night, Emily had dinner waiting on him, as usual, but she couldn't think of eating anything herself. She tried to seem as happy as she'd been at the store when they said goodbye and hoped he wouldn't notice that anything had changed. He told her that he got the day off, like they wanted, and she told him she was excited to go shopping.

"Then why are you so dreary?" He cocked an eyebrow her way.

"I'm not dreary." She snapped a little and tried to restrain the defensiveness in her voice. "I took Red on a long walk today."

"You shouldn't wander too much. It isn't safe."

"Nothing happened. Nothing important anyway." She decided it was better to escape the conversation than lie to him further. "I think I'll turn in early, so I can be awake for our date."

"Is it a date?" Todd said, bemused.

"I've heard that's what happens when people like each other."

"We can call it a date."

7

They got to the mall about 10:30 and it was mostly dead. The glass doors were unlocked, but the inside was a mausoleum, dark and silent. Many of the metal security screens were pulled down in front of shops, and there was no power. Since there weren't really any windows either except the entrance doors, they immediately turned on the large camp lanterns they'd brought from home. There were no sales people, no customers except the two of them.

"It's so sad." Even though she spoke softly, her voice bounced around in the space. "Why have so many places closed?"

Todd shrugged. "A lot of stuff didn't survive the recession I guess. I mean that's why SolarStar closed."

He didn't sound confident in his answer, and she thought, he'd never admit it, but he was probably feeling as strange in that empty space as she did. "Right. I didn't think of that."

She stood there, a statue of wonder and sadness, looking around at the dark signs of the nearby stores. There was an old camera place that did repairs, some kind of kitchen supply place where they sold quirky kitchen décor. She thought about seeing if she could open the gate, because they probably had some of the cow stuff she collected, but Todd had agreed to take her shopping for clothes, not another kitchen cow. When she didn't move, Todd tried to sound cheerful. "So where do you want to shop?"

"I don't know." She peered through the dark window of a jewelry store, but there was no one inside and even the diamonds were dull in the unlit cases. Emily didn't wear a wedding band. She couldn't remember why. She knew Todd had bought her one once, a little diamond solitaire shaped like a teardrop. She didn't even know where the ring had ended up, but Todd wore his wedding band, and she supposed that was good enough for both of them.

By degrees, they meandered deeper into the empty mall, their footsteps seemingly louder on the floor the deeper into the darkness they went. Emily wandered through one or two stores she thought she remembered liking once but didn't see anything that felt both practical and beautiful as her tastes seemed lately to run. She didn't even try anything on; she just flipped through racks and stacks of clothes.

"Why do you do that?"

"Do what?"

"Look through everything on the rack. They

put everything together. The shirt behind the shirt is the same shirt."

"Not always," Emily said stubbornly. "Sometimes they do them by color, or the style varies slightly."

"So...the same shirt...only in a different color." Todd turned away, she suspected, to avoid her seeing him roll his eyes.

Todd didn't understand the difference between a sweater and a cardigan any more than she understood why farts were funny. By the third store, Todd had already had his fill of shopping. He started sighing with impatience and throwing his weight periodically from one foot to another. He didn't say he wanted to leave of course, because he'd gotten himself into the position of having to take her shopping and would never admit such a defeat. The feeling, however, was completely mutual. If he'd said he'd wanted to leave, she might have immediately walked out of the store, not because she'd had enough shopping, but because she'd had quite enough of him.

There were some things that no quantity of snickerdoodles could repair, like Todd's pissy attitude and her inability to stop poking the bear. She felt lonely again, especially in the deserted space of the mall, and wished she'd brought Red along for the trip. The dog at least would have shown some enthusiasm. It was sad, she thought, that Todd didn't have as much patience as her dog and wasn't half as trainable. She felt bad for thinking that, but not bad enough not to think it again.

Especially after the fourth store they entered, by which time Todd was practically out of his mind fidgeting. "Come on, Em. Just pick something. I said I'd take you shopping, not looking for a fucking unicorn."

Emily glared at him over a rack of sweaters. "You have a funny way of apologizing."

"Christ." Todd pinched the bridge of his nose but said nothing more, at least not loud enough for her to hear and call him on.

They trudged up the unmoving escalator to the second floor of the mall. Most of the stores there she passed because they were candle shops or make-up counters or beauty salons. It seemed like there were even more shut up stores on the second floor than there had been on the first, and one or two that she might have gone in were locked up tight. Finally, they found a store called Tooley's that Emily couldn't remember ever going in before. It looked like the kind of place where high school girls shopped. There was a skateboard hanging in the window by the mannequin, who was dressed like it was thinking about going clubbing. She hadn't the slightest idea why someone would need a skateboard for that activity and wondered what half-brained sales person had put together the ridiculous display. There was little chance of finding anything worthwhile inside. She went in anyway, mostly because it annoyed Todd to keep shopping, and, other than finding some new jeans that didn't sag around her hips, annoying Todd was the second most important thing in the world.

To her surprise, there were quite a few nice things in the store that didn't seem too young or too flashy. They were all junior's sizes, but she guessed that after losing enough weight to warrant new jeans anyway, she probably didn't have to worry about them fitting. Before long, she'd loaded herself up and Todd like twin camels and headed for the dressing room in the back.

She hung the camp lantern from one of the clothing hooks and the clothes on the other hooks inside the dressing room. Then she handed Todd her purse.

He stared at it like it was made of lizards and filled with bubonic plague. "Seriously?"

"Take it." She thrust the purse toward him.

Todd took the bag like it was radioactive. "Why can't you just take it in?"

"I'm already taking in the backpack. There's only so much room in there. Besides, there's no one here. What possible threat could there be to your vast ego in an empty store?""

"Fine." Todd flopped down on a pouf placed outside the dressing rooms for just such an occasion, sinking into it much more than he clearly expected, and he wrapped both arms around her purse, covering as much of it with his body as possible.

"There you go." Emily grinned. "Guard it with your life."

She lost track of time putting on and pulling off clothes, but a while later she'd narrowed down a few prime choices she liked the best. One blue shirt was very flattering. Emily pulled it off and dropped it into the open backpack sitting in the corner. The small dressing room had powder pink carpet and smelled a little like feet, and she was feeling strangely lonely with only herself to look at in the mirror. "Do you think Mr. Ward and Mrs. Aims are having an affair?"

Outside the fitting room, Todd laughed. "Not unless there's a lot of Viagra involved."

"Gross, Todd. I don't want to think about that." Emily reached for the jeans slung over the dressing room door. They had little swirls of stitching on the pockets shaped like butterfly wings. She had mixed feelings about them. She liked the style but was unsure what use there was to having butterfly wings on her butt. "I mean, it could have been an affair of the heart. Maybe they're totally in love."

"I don't know." She could hear amusement and boredom mingling in his voice. "Maybe. Are you almost done?"

She glared at the dressing room door and

hoped he'd feel it. "Don't rush me."

"Sorry dear." He sighed, obnoxiously loud. "Shutting up."

"I am almost done." She smiled at the thought of Todd in irritation sitting on the zebra striped poof outside the dressing room, holding her purse and surrounded by women's clothing and dainty things, but she frowned when she looked into the mirror. Between her pristine white bra and panties was a wasteland of wrinkly skin. It had always been bad, at least as long as she remembered, but it was getting worse the more weight she lost.

She ran her hands over her protruding ribs and a dull pink scar that ran across her lower abdomen, then turned slightly to examine the sad, flabby state of ass affairs. "Awful."

Outside the door, Todd groaned. "You want me to get you a different pair?"

She was too distracted by how cruddy she looked to be mad at him for his impatience this time. "No. They fit. I'm just too skinny."

"You look fine, dear."

Emily squeezed the loose skin of her stomach with two fingers. "You have to say that. You're my husband. I wish-"

Emily stopped and closed her eyes for a vision that stole her away, a thief in the dark of her brain. A dark-haired woman, pressing a coffee mug to her lips, the edges of her mouth curled and catty. Laughter, raucous. Girlish fear. If they didn't tone it down, they'd be asked to leave. They were too happy to allow the artsy types brood properly. Honesty, brutal but loving, even in the worst pair of jeans. How long had it been? She shook her head, trying to scatter the woman's face across the floor where it wouldn't hurt her anymore. She felt sick, the kind of deep heartsick that turned the floor into a waterbed and made her unsteady on her feet.

"Emily?"

The sound of Todd's voice at least steadied the floor. There was no telling how long she'd been quiet. "I'm fine." The words rushed out because she wanted to believe them, and quietly, because she didn't want to hear them sound untrue. She pulled the jeans on with ease and didn't bother with another butt check. No one cared about her butt, or whether it had butterfly wings, not even her. Her stomach felt like it was full of coffee grounds and cottage cheese, and she wanted to go home. She couldn't remember ever having wanted to be at home that much before. She had the jeans around her knees when Todd called to her again.

"Emily." This time the tone of his voice bored into her with alarm. Something was wrong, and not just that wrong thing clunking around inside her brain. There was a low moan, a clatter, a loud crash, a rack hitting the floor, and hangers scattering across the carpet. Emily jerked the jeans up to her waist and fastened the top button without bothering with the zipper. "Todd?"

No response but grunting, and that wasn't only coming from Todd.

Emily reached into the backpack for the .45 she'd thrown in next to tampons and lip moisturizer. She pushed open the dressing room door, stepped into the dark shop still wearing nothing but the jeans and her bra. The lamp behind her cast a long beam of dim light across the floor, filled by her silhouette. Todd was on his back, straining to keep the girl's snapping teeth from his exposed neck and face.

The girl was quite pretty, except for the oozing bite on her arm and black veins festering under pale grey skin. Her nametag said "Sara" and she had smoldering red hair that curled wildly around her face. Her head was bloody on one side where someone had failed to hit her properly the first time, and her mouth was bloody for probably the same reason. Emily rolled her eyes at the incompetence of Sara's last customer, at the same moment, she realized the girl was wearing the exact pair of jeans Emily had just put on in the dressing room but filled out the butt butterflies much better.

"Emily!"

"I've got her, Todd." She rolled her eyes again, gripped the gun with both hands, and pulled the trigger. Red hair, black blood, and grey brain splattered onto a purple T-Shirt that said, "Espresso Yourself" in scrolling silver letters.

Todd pushed Sara's limp body into the floor and slowly climbed to his feet. They said nothing for a moment while he bent over to recover himself. "Pushy sales people." He fumbled for the words between breaths.

"Uh-huh." She stared at him expectantly.

He closed his eyes and hunched his shoulders forward. "I know."

"One teenage girl Todd?"

"I said I know."

She didn't know whether she wanted to laugh or scream at him. Emily grabbed her old shirt from the dressing room floor and pulled it on, then grabbed the backpack, zipped the gun inside with her new clothes, and tossed it over her one shoulder. She sat the camp light down on the floor while she retied her shoes. "What did you do with my purse?"

Todd cringed. "I think it's got brain on it."

"Damnit, Todd."

But she was derailed from chastising him further. They were still shopping, after all, and there was a whole rack of brain-free purses behind the sales counter. Todd said nothing while she opened and looked inside each one until she found one that she liked slightly more than the old. Then he waited patiently while she carefully took her things out of the disgusting purse and transferred them over to the new one. "I'm done shopping. I want to go home."

She knew he wouldn't argue with her. But he had his wallet in his hand, standing by the register. "How much do we owe them?"

Emily almost went to check the tags, but she stopped herself. "I don't think we owe them anything."

"You're just going to take all that stuff?"

"Yeah. I think I am. With service that bad, they deserve to be robbed."

Todd looked at her like she was a stranger, and was clearly uncomfortable with robbing the store, but he followed her silently out into tomb of the mall.

8

Red was happy to see them when they got home. She was almost worried he'd be pouty, but he greeted them at the door and did a dance of joyful circles around them, as though he thought they might not have ever come home again. She sat down on the floor and let him climb all over her while she petted him. Then she went upstairs, where she put on all the new clothes again, so she could show them to Todd. Todd looked away from the television long enough to tell her she looked nice. He did not notice the butt butterflies at all, and by the time she'd finished her fashion show, she felt worse from his lackluster compliments than if he hadn't looked at her all. It was a terrible thing to be seen and ignored all at once.

Eventually, she sat down on one end of the sofa and welcomed as much of Red as would fit in her lap. He'd been clinging to her heels ever since she got home, so much so that she was determined not to leave the house without him again, even if she was going somewhere he wasn't allowed.

She didn't want to watch Todd's movie,

which was something about a guy falling in love with a fat girl and how that was somehow both shocking and funny. It was all a little disgusting, and she was perturbed that Todd was so in to it. She wondered if she got fat if he'd leave her, but that was a stupid thought.

Todd wouldn't need her to be fat to leave. She wasn't sure why he stuck around at all. She stared at the television anyway, because there was nothing else to do. In her head, there was a different story, one made all the more intriguing by her inability to recall it.

The girl she remembered in the dressing room, Emily was certain she had known her once. The image had been too real for her crappy imagination, and the colors, even the sounds, were vivid enough to make her think that there was something important about that woman that cowered on the edges of her mind like a child in the dark. As Emily thought of her, she felt a connection that seemed to stretch through and drop anchor in empty space.

"Emily?"

She blinked and looked at Todd. "What?"

He sat with the remote in his hand, both eyebrows raised, and his chin dipped down like he was staring at her over some invisible pair of eyeglasses. "The movie is over."

She'd been staring at an empty screen. "I know." She had no idea why she lied about that, except that she didn't want to talk, to be forced to tell him about a girl she could barely remember only to have him accuse her of imagining things again. If he'd left her alone, she might have gone back to staring at the empty screen and trying to fill in the mystery in her mind.

Todd huffed and set the remote down on the sofa beside him. "What's wrong?"

"Nothing." Red had fallen asleep. She ran one of his silky yellow ears between two fingers, and let it flop back against this head.

"Seriously." Todd's face was exasperated. "What did I do now?"

"Nothing, Todd. Not every thought in my head has to be about you."

"Was I not paying close enough attention to your clothes?"

She rolled her eyes and leaned her head against the backrest of the sofa. "I said it wasn't about you."

"I'm worried about you."

She looked at him and thought of just telling him about the girl, but honesty was overruled in favor of self-defense. "I'm fine."

"That's like, the last thing you should say if you want me to believe you're fine. I'm fine is universal chick language for 'I'm pissed and it's your fault.'"

She tried to smile at him, stretching her face like putty that only held shape for a moment.

"Since when do you know so much about women Todd? The next thing I know, you'll be wanting to talk about my periods."

Todd scrunched his nose and squirmed on the sofa. "Just because I know it exists doesn't mean I want to talk about it."

Todd was still staring at her. She thought there was little chance of distracting him outside of talking about lady functions. Red was like an inferno in her lap, but he was far too cute to move. She rubbed his ears absently and looked down at the carpet. "I just thought of something earlier is all. It bothered me a little, and I've been thinking about it since."

Todd looked slightly relieved. "Well what was it?"

Emily sighed. "I don't know if I want to talk about it."

"Maybe I can help you figure it out. Did you remember a dream or something? Sometimes you have nightmares."

Emily shook her head. "It wasn't a dream. I think it was a memory." She watched Todd's face carefully. His look shifted from one of base curiosity to real concern. "Did I used to know a girl with long brown hair? I feel like I did."

Todd frowned. "I don't know. Why would you think about that?"

"I don't know why I thought about her, but I did. I was standing in the dressing room and she popped into my head."

Todd rubbed his hand over the back of his neck, like he suddenly had pain there. "Seriously, Em. I'm trying to help you, but you've got to help me a little. I mean, first you see things at the dump, and now you're dreaming people up in the living room. You need to get hold of yourself. I don't know what to do for you if you're just going to keep heading toward crazy at every turn."

"I'm not crazy, Todd. I remember her laughing and drinking coffee. Why would my imagination just make up some random girl drinking coffee? She had to be real."

"Uh-huh, and so was the guy in the dump because the dog said so."

Red lifted his head off her lap and raised an offended eyebrow at Todd that she thought exemplified exactly how she felt. He laid down again with a snort. Emily appreciated his attempt to stand up for her but wished dogs had words instead of only nasty glances.

"When you put it like that, of course I sound completely crazy, but that's just it isn't it. You can't really talk to me, so you just assume everything I say is garbage you don't have to listen to because it's crazy."

Todd chewed on his lip in exasperation. "I'm listening to you right now, Em. And you sound crazy."

Emily looked away from him, back at the

empty television. "Because you're not really listening. I'm only half here to you, like a ghost."

He didn't really answer her. It was clear all he wanted was to get the conversation over with. "Fine. Whatever. You remember some girl. I don't know. Maybe you knew her before we met."

She was getting infinitely tired of his eye rolls. "Sure. That makes perfect sense."

"Okay then."

"Yeah. I'm glad." She pushed Red off her lap and climbed from the sofa. "I'd hate to say anything that didn't make complete sense. I might break you. It might shatter your universe to think that not everything has to make perfect sense."

Todd huffed and closed his eyes. "I'm not going to fight with you about some girl you think you remember. I told you I don't know, and I don't know why you're pissed at me for not being able to read your mind."

"I'm not pissed at you." She said, but in her brain, there was more to say. '*I'm done with you.*' But she'd never be able to say that much out loud. More importantly, she thought he was lying, and she felt that there was always something in him that seemed a little disingenuous. Even when he told her the truth he sounded like he was trying to slip something by her. He never looked trustworthy, fidgeting on the sofa, flicking one of the plastic buttons on the remote control with the edge of his fingernail, like he had something to hide.

But he had no reason to lie about this, and if she read too much into it, she'd be guilty of the crazy he so often accused her of. The memory, in the grand scheme of the world, was so inane. So irrelevant. There was no benefit for him to lie about it and irritate her so much. He had nothing to gain. She couldn't stand to look at him, to think about him anymore. "Goodnight, Todd." She spun for the stairs and stomped away.

"Yeah." She heard him mutter. As she climbed the stairs with Red beside her, she heard Todd put in another DVD.

9

That night, she dreamed about the girl again. The memory wasn't that much different from a dream. It was the same girl with the same long, wavy hair. She had the same laugh, and the same smile that made her eyes crinkle at the edges. Her eyes were speckled hazel. That much, Emily hadn't noticed before. But there was one new piece, the feel of their warm cheeks pressed together, smiling, and a flash.

She woke up before Todd went to work but pretended to be sleeping as he got ready to leave. She didn't want her face to betray that she remembered something more, and whatever she had with the woman she remembered, it was something that had then been all their own. Todd would never understand it. He would only call her crazy for having any emotion at all. Emily refused to share this, to share her, with him anymore; she didn't belong to him.

Sometime in the night's restlessness, she'd developed a plan, and it was present in her mind as she listened to Todd mill about that morning. If she remembered taking a photograph with the woman in her dream, then photographic evidence might exist somewhere to prove that she was sane. If she could only find something, she might have more to go on than a fragment of glass floating in water.

When Todd finally left, she opened her eyes and looked around the walls. There were no pictures in the bedroom except art she'd purchased to match the décor, which was a pale sage with silver accents. The art was abstract, and she'd never seen it as being as particularly useless as it seemed. She couldn't remember herself as the woman who thought some sage smudges on canvas was a worthwhile purchase. There was little reality to it; the walls felt alien, like they belonged in some other house on a different planet.

She climbed out of bed, and Red followed her out the bedroom door. There were no pictures in the upstairs hallway. This she'd covered with the same cream color as the downstairs, and though there was a framed still life of yellow daisies, there was nothing personal about them, except that she enjoyed the color of the flower. She ran her hand along bare paint and plaster, and at first everything seemed as empty as she remembered.

But then, by chance, she found a few small, unpatched nail holes that might once have had hanging pictures. It was difficult to tell. She stepped back from the wall and stared at it resolutely. Slowly, she made out the shape of the frame. The picture might have been gone, but there was a slight difference in color where the frame had protected the wall from dirt. She couldn't remember what had been hanging there. She couldn't remember hanging anything at all, but the house was new when they bought it. It wasn't something someone else had left behind.

She drifted down the stairs, feeling and looked around for more conclusive evidence. The formal room felt the same as their bedroom, cold and foreign. From the extra lock on the door, to the boarded window, to a shelf filled with curios of abstract glass and fake potted plants, there was not a single personal memento.

But there were more holes in the walls. Once she thought to look for them they seemed to jump out in every bare space. Even before she cut through the kitchen and in to the family room, she knew it would be the same. There was her collection of cows in the kitchen, which she had, at that moment, developed a seething hatred of, but there was nothing personal. In the family room, a table set for four, with a wicker basket filled with glass balls in a bright blue, the sofa, the television, Todd's ridiculous DVD collection that took up nearly an entire wall, and a painting of a sunny beach that seemed positively frigid.

She pushed both hands through her hair and pulled in disbelief, seeing the house she lived in for what felt like the first time. It was her, but it wasn't. She remembered putting that cut out of a wooden cow just over the stove and arranging the balls in the basket with more care than that task probably called for, but this wasn't the house she made or remembered.

She would have hung up a photo of their wedding, something from their honeymoon, pictures of friends, or family, or . . .

She would never have left the house so barren and cold. In a rush of certainty, she came to the only conclusion available, she hadn't. If not pictures on the wall, she would have kept albums, at least, but there wasn't a single album in any cabinet or drawer. She lived in a house of nothing.

It felt like a cave or a cage that she'd disguised as a house to distract from what it was, and without a single photograph, she felt she'd never find the key to let herself out again. She stood at the foot of the stairs and looked up at the bare carpet and naked walls to the white door at the top of the stairs.

Todd said it was storage, but he always seemed dishonest. Maybe he lied about that door too, though she couldn't imagine why he'd want to keep her away from it.

She hesitated, one foot on the bottom stair, half thinking that she should leap them two at a time and throw open that door to see what was inside. The other half, was rooted to the floor, trying to convince her that none of this was true. Todd was the only one who could have taken away the pictures, and he never went in the upstairs rooms either. Like her, he always walked by without really seeing those doors. How much, and for how long, had she been this blind?

Red scratched at the back door, interrupting her internal argument. He probably just wanted to crap, but he helped her all the same. Todd had boxes in the shed. Except for retrieving the garden tools, she never went inside. There were always spiders lurking in the back corners and she was perpetually paranoid that they would find her hair a fantastic place to land. She was pretty sure some of them were venomous, but since they never really went back there it seemed easiest just to live and let web.

She slid open the back door and followed Red who burst out into the yard. She hesitated again at the door of the shed. It was like she was looking at a black hole and stretching slowly into spaghetti, but she took a deep breath and pulled the door open to let in the light. There were more boxes than she remembered being there, but she couldn't trust her memory. They had always been there, she just never paid attention. But now that she was seeing more clearly, even the boxes didn't make sense. Even if she couldn't remember what was in them, why would Todd have put them out in the shed with the spiders if they had so many rooms for storage upstairs. Most of the boxes had Todd's name scrawled in his childish handwriting across the sides and top.

It only took ten minutes of spider dodging and box shuffling to find what she wanted. At the back of the shed, in a large, warped, and weather stained box near the bottom, she found what remained of their lives. There were loose photographs and four photo albums yellowing from exposure to the temperatures and warping from the moisture outside. There was another box of framed photographs, which she assumed she had once hung in the house. Todd hadn't even taken care to keep them whole before he threw them in the shed, and many of the frames were broken and the pictures scratched from shards of glass.

The sight of everything so withered and broken was too much like the feeling that permeated her chest; as much as those pictures had represented her life before, they did even more so now in their deterioration. She sat crying in the grass, running her fingers over album covers, broken glass, and curling picture edges.

Slowly she spread everything out on the grass and tried to draw it into herself all at once, but she only created a sea of faces to get lost in. Strangers remained strangers, and even those pictures with her in them, arm in arm or leaning in, were unbelievably unreal, like she was a voyeur of someone else's life. She swiped the photographs into a wave with her forearm and reached for the photo albums. Page by page, she studied every face, and each new page added to the crushing weight of the unfamiliar.

There were pictures of hiking trips to at least three different countries, piles of parties, and stacks of girls squashing together to fit in the frame. She thought for so long that she lived a life so ordinary as to forget it all, that she remembered nothing because nothing was worth remembering, but all the evidence ink and paper could provide proved she had once been adventurous, popular, and loved. She suffocated in the open air, barely drawing breath.

There were no pictures of the girl anywhere, not even in the background, and she might have been shattered by disappointment if she hadn't noticed that there were no pictures of Todd either. There were still no wedding photos, and it was impossible that they had never once found a reason to be photographed together. Those other pictures had to still exist. Even Todd, with his callousness and indifference would never go so far as to destroy such important pieces of their lives.

Emily dried her eyes with her hands, which smelled like salt and grass. Once again, she braved the shed and dug through every box and cobweb, but there were no more pictures to be found. Instead, she found boxes of junk that might as well have been carted off to the dump. Sadness became desperation, and desperation, like most of her other emotions, shifted quickly into lividity.

But anger was a blessing. Todd might have taken all the pictures away, but no matter how much he tried to erase, he couldn't take away her brain. She still had her mind, and justice was that her memories of him could serve as the foundation for others.

He at least was not a stranger, even when she felt she didn't know him. She remembered marrying him. She remembered his tuxedo and his cornflower blue tie. She remembered walking toward him down the aisle and saying all those meaningful words, and her bouquet, soft blue and white hydrangea tied with a ribbon that she'd handed off to hold on to Todd.

Emily closed her eyes and drifted down the aisle in her mind. She saw everything but Todd through smoke. The whole room whirled with fog, but even a clouded image was better than nothing at all. She could see the groomsmen, their bowties the same color as the blue flowers in her bouquet, and the bridesmaid's dresses, simple but beautiful, with lovely clips that sparkled in their hair. Her maid of honor, with her beautiful long brown hair swept up behind her head.

Like the wind had come at last, she saw the

girl's face, her hazel eyes, the same mischief living at the corners of them.

Danny. Emily struggled, no. Danielle, but she'd always been Danny since high school, because there were four other girls in their class named Danielle. Danny wanted to be unique, and she was. She didn't need to change her name. She was loyal, spontaneous, hilarious. Every boy had chased after Danny, but Danny didn't care for any of them, because she liked girls, but didn't say so until college, when she first introduced Emily to her girlfriend.

Danny had called Emily her other girlfriend, and said they were soul mates and nothing would come between them. The other girl had been jealous, but it was never that way, because Emily and Danny were like sisters, they shared something deeper than blood. Emily choked on sorrow and guilt. How could she have forgotten so much love?

Red stopped his frolic and came to see what the matter with her was. She tried to push him away, but he was determined. He put a paw on her shoulder to steady himself on his hind legs and forcibly licked her face. The weight of him forced her back into the grass, where she was at the mercy of his disgusting breath and wet tongue. But it was at least a fraction of love again. She wrapped her arms around his neck and sobbed into his yellow fur, he rested against her, content to be her pillow and her tissue and to let her soak his fur.

She might have been content to lay there all day and let unhappiness march over her and sweep her away, but it couldn't last. From the yard next door, Mr. Johnson moaned.

Emily sat up, scowling at the block wall between the yards, and angrily wiped her eyes. "Everything's okay Mr. Johnson." She had to force happiness into her at mental gunpoint.

Mr. Johnson only moaned in disbelief.

"Really, there's nothing wrong. I'll be fine." She swept the pictures up into her arms and hurried inside the house before he interrupted her misery again.

10

She made Todd dinner that day but wasn't sure if she'd let him eat it or throw the whole plate in his face. She had to try to restrain herself though, because in between sorting through pictures and cooking, in the empty hours of her day, she'd had too much time to think. What she needed was not just to be angry at Todd, she needed to figure out his game. Except for plain cruelty she couldn't think of a single reason why he'd go out of his way to erase her life after she'd lost her memory, but he'd done it. If she threw a plate at his forehead the minute he came through the door, she'd probably never find out the truth. She needed to be patient, to let him lie.

When she heard the front door click, she moved to stand in the passage between the kitchen and the family room. Todd looked like he'd had a busy day. There were dark stains on his trousers, but no part of her was willing to wait for him to rest up or even settle in. She damn well wasn't going to wait for a good day; there would never be one.

As usual, Todd had no sense of when he

was dangling a foot in the lion's cage, and he bent down to kiss her as though she'd been standing there waiting for that purpose. She let him kiss her but was barely able to tolerate him in the sanctity of her personal space. When she spoke, her voice sounded like she'd been using her vocal chords to grate cheese. "How was your day?"

"The usual. Kind of slow."

She nodded and stepped away, eager to put space between them and avoid being so close he could read the thoughts behind her face. "My day was slow too."

He lifted an eyebrow. "Don't you always have slow days?"

"Yes. I was just making conversation. Dinner is ready, if you're hungry."

"Great."

She handed him a plate. She had already fed Red, but she made nothing for herself. "I did do one thing today."

He held the plate with both hands, like a child who'd been told not to spill.

"I thought of something."

"You've got too much time to think."

"It was only a small thing." She watched him. On the surface, he seemed completely relaxed, and she might have believed it was true except that she had his devoted attention, which he wouldn't have given her if he wasn't worried about what she would say. He said nothing, undoubtedly trying to avoid asking her what it was she thought of, which only made her want to tell him more. "You remember that girl I asked about?"

"Yeah. I still don't know her."

"I didn't say you did, but I remembered more. I remembered her name."

"Is that all?" Todd was so casual, but he stared at the dinner plate in his hands like the gravy was going to spring up and suck on his face.

"Danny." She watched to see if the word shook him. If he felt anything at all, she couldn't tell. "The girl I was thinking of. Her name is Danny."

Todd shuffled his weight from one foot to the other, but it seemed more like impatience than guilt. "Okay."

"You don't remember her?"

He glowered. "I told you no."

She wanted to bore into him and pull the truth out with both hands, but she had more restraint than she expected. "I thought you might now that I remembered her name." She shrugged, like the thing that mattered most to her in the world at that moment didn't matter at all.

The action seemed to disarm him. He wasn't on edge anymore. "Still no. I was never close with your friends. That was always your thing. Maybe I met her once, but I don't remember. I don't know what else to tell you.

What's for dinner?"

He was lying. He was doing a good job of hiding it, but she was sure. "It's. . . beef stew." He wasn't even going to let that much of his game go by unplayed.

"Sounds great." He held the plate with one hand; its contents slid slowly to the edge. "I got some new movies."

She noticed for the first time he had a plastic bag tucked under one arm. "I'd rather not. I'm tired of movies. It seems like all we ever do."

She felt him trying to peel up her layers and look inside. It was uncomfortable, but this time, he'd never reach the center and find out that she knew more than she let on. She turned her back to him under the pretense of cleaning, unsure how much longer she could suppress her rage without showing him it was there, but her voice came out singsong and overtly pleasant, despite the lines of effort dug into her face. "Do you remember our wedding, Todd?"

"Yeah, I guess so."

"You guess so?" She scoffed, but to her relief, it sounded more playful than scornful. "I hope that's not a thing you'd just forget."

"It's been a while."

She hated the simplicity of his answer, the total nonchalance where he seemed to live most days. He had no idea how much it hurt her, how the lies were so much worse when it seemed effortless for him. "It feels like a lifetime."

Todd cleared his throat. "I thought that was kind of the point."

Humor too, it was funny to him not to tell the truth. She did her best to force a bit of laughter from her throat. "Yeah, I guess so."

"What got you thinking about that?"

"Oh, I don't know. It was just a thought."

She heard him set the stew plate down on the counter. "I remember your dress was like, fluffy on the bottom, and sleeveless. It was pretty on you."

"Thanks." She managed through grinding teeth while she scrubbed the counter with excessive force.

"You were mad about the frosting. It was the wrong shade of blue. You were tromping around the hotel complaining that the cake decorator didn't know the difference between cornflower and periwinkle, and it was funny. I thought, no one on the planet knows the difference between those two colors except for you. We danced to that song you liked, even though the DJ only had the crappy country version instead of rock."

So much detail. He thought he was appeasing her with these pleasant memories, and some deep part of her was gratified that he remembered so many stupid little things. But that same comfort made his efforts to hide the larger things seem much worse. If he could remember something as useless as cornflower and periwinkle, he must have remembered bigger things too. She turned to look at him again. He was standing with his hands in his pockets. "Anything else?"

"I don't know, Em. We said some words, had some cake, danced, and left. It was a wedding. They're all the same." He picked up his bowl again. "What do you remember?" His voice was too casual, his body deliberately lax.

She shrugged and looked down at Red who had spent the day at her feet. "I should really get him some normal dog food."

"Em." His voice had that fatherly tone she hated. "Don't change the subject."

"I don't remember anything important. I remember getting married, but you're right. They're all the same. I was just thinking about it today. It's weird we don't have any pictures. That doesn't seem normal."

Todd dipped his chin. "I'm sure we do. They're probably just boxed up somewhere. I'll look for them this weekend if you want."

"Sure. It would be fun to see them."

"Do you want me to get your dog some food on the way home or something?"

Far too accommodating. Todd wasn't the type to go out of his way for anything, especially not for a dog he didn't even want. He was trying to placate her with dog food, and he thought so little of her that he was certain it would work. She smiled while seething. "If you don't mind; it would save me a trip, but I can do it."

"I'll do it." He said quickly. "Tomorrow."

"Thanks." The fight to stay smiling against the gloom physically hurt her face.

"Sure."

Todd looked as though he wanted permission to leave, but she wasn't ready for him to go just yet. "Who was your best man? I can't remember."

Todd stared straight at the kitchen tile, his lips downturned like melting wax. "It was Scott." The words seemed to hurt him. "My brother."

"That's right," she chirped. "I forgot you even had a brother. You guys used to be really close I think."

"We were." Todd swallowed. "Before." He took a deep breath, and his shoulders shuddered. "We don't talk much anymore." Todd snatched his plate and went into the family room. Emily sat down on the tile and petted Red. He wasn't opposed to the floor; he was as happy in her lap there as he was anywhere else.

Todd was lying. She was sure, but how much was lie, she couldn't be certain. The fact that he felt the need to appease her with dog food and weekend chores was enough to prove that he felt at least a little guilty. She suspected he knew right where the pictures were and had put them away on purpose, but she couldn't imagine why he'd go to so much trouble to hide something she must have eventually noticed was missing.

And he remembered so much about the wedding. He remembered his brother as the best man, but not Danny as her maid of honor. It would have been impossible for Emily not to seek out Danny's approval before marrying him in the first place. At minimum, they met at the wedding, but more probably, they'd spent extended time together, and Todd was deliberately avoiding the existence of anything they'd been before.

Of course, she'd forgotten Todd had a brother, but he said himself, they didn't talk much anymore, and she obviously didn't talk to Danny anymore. But there was no reason for that. They hadn't had a fight. As far as Emily knew, they never really fought, and she felt that even if they didn't see each other for months, they were the kind of friends that time wouldn't diminish. By the time she climbed up from the floor, she had made up her mind to try something that was probably impossible. Tomorrow, she would take Red for another car ride.

11

She wasn't exactly sure where she was going, and that was always a bad idea. There were accidents and abandoned cars, and sometimes groups of people blocking the road protesting or walking for some fundraising cause and disrupting traffic. She was hoping that if she just broke up her normal routine, which really only consisted of the path between home and the hardware store or the dump, she might see something that jogged her memory. It probably wasn't a good idea to let instinct drive the car, but she tried to think as little as possible and just enjoy the ride at least a tenth as much as Red enjoyed letting his ears flap outside the window.

She had to make some unfamiliar turns. There was a military vehicle overturned in one street, but there weren't many people around, which was a relief. She nearly got lost cutting through a subdivision that she was pretty sure had been modeled after the master plan of inescapable hell, but when she came out onto a main road again, she knew exactly where she was. Every street sign and mailbox were splashes of familiarity. The last three turns, one down

Gracechurch Road, another on 115th avenue, and the last onto Danny's street, she made from memory.

Danny's neighborhood was unusually crowded considering that it wasn't yet noon. The houses here were older than those in the subdivision where Emily and Todd lived. The neighborhood was rougher. Some of the houses had been remodeled and updated at various points, but some of them were questionable looking, with tin foil covering some of the windows and graffiti on the garage doors. The lack of a homeowner's association meant that people could basically do what they wanted, and as a result, at least one person on the block had thought that neon pink was a good shade for shutters on a green house.

She thought someone must have been having a party because the street was filled with cars, and people milled about between them as if they weren't sure where to go. Rather than pull down closer and risk getting hemmed in by traffic, she parked at the end of the street. Red was looking out all the windows and occasionally back at Emily like he wasn't sure she was in the best frame of mind. But he was up for an adventure, and his tail wagged as he crawled to the driver's seat and leapt onto the pavement. They made their way quickly through the lawns to Danny's front door. Some of the neighbors noticed that there were new people around, and Red circled Emily's feet like a yellow sidewalk shark. Emily knocked softly, trying not to draw too much more attention, but there was no answer. She didn't have time to wait. Danny's neighbors were on the verge of being too friendly, beginning to wander in her direction. Red had his mohawk going on; Emily tried the door, but it was locked.

She sighed, hardly in the mood for feats of athleticism, but she didn't have much choice. She moved for the side of the house and told Red to wait for her. She climbed the fence, which was fortunately easier than she anticipated because it was made of wood supported by metal crossbeams that were just big enough to accommodate the toe of her shoe. When she landed with a little grunt in Danny's back yard, she was happy to see the key stuck in the padlock of the gate. She unlocked it to let Red through, and then locked it again, so she could keep nosy neighbors in the realm of their own damn business. The key she put in her pocket. It wasn't safe to leave it sitting there. Anyone could let themselves through.

Danny had let the landscaping go. She'd never had Emily's green thumb, but it looked like she hadn't watered the yard or plucked a weed in decades. Red pounced playfully through the high weeds, but the yard made Emily feel barren. She couldn't be sure because her memories were so full of holes, but she felt as though Danny wasn't the type of person to let something like this go. Emily turned from the yard to stare at the back of the house. All the curtains and blinds were drawn, except the one over the sliding door. Emily looked inside to a dark kitchen and small dining room. Danny's style was much richer than Emily's, with dark woods and grey granite, where Emily had sunshine and daisies. And yet they were such friends. A few generations ago, Danny's family had been from Italy, and that heritage was dripping from every aspect of Danny's house. Emily remembered eating shrimp pasta at that dining room table, and the thought of it made her hungrier than she had been in a quite a long time.

The sliding door was locked too. Emily knocked on the glass with two knuckles. It took a few breathless minutes, but she came. Danny shuffled across the tile, leaving black half-moon footprints in a trail behind her. Her hair was just what Emily remembered, except it hadn't been brushed and was knotted up on one side of Danny's face. The hazel eyes Emily had seen dancing with laughter in her mind were dim and rimmed with streaks of red. Her veins were black and distended, causing her to look older than she really was, and her nightgown had a blood-stained hole in one side that shifted when she moved and showed the grey flesh and bare bone beneath.

"Hi Danny." Her voice wasn't loud enough

to carry through the door, but Danny seemed to hear her all the same. Danny tilted her head to one side and took another step toward the glass door. Red growled.

"No, Red." She reached down to pet his ears, but her eyes were locked on her friend inside the house. "This is Danny. She's okay. She's. . . she was my best friend."

Danny pressed her face against the glass; her lips were pulled back away from her teeth and her gums were dry, her tongue shriveled. Emily leaned her forehead against the cool glass too, so that thin pane was the only thing that kept them apart. "I missed you, Danny, even when I didn't realize you were gone. Nothing has been the same. Nothing will ever be the same without you."

Danny pressed a grey hand against the glass, almost like she could understand, like she could want to reach out and touch Emily as much for the pleasure of seeing her as for sickness and hunger. Emily pressed her hand there too, and looked into Danny's sad eyes, looking for more signs of the girl she knew, but there was nothing. The real Danny was gone, but Emily spoke to her anyway, hoping that the words would sink through. "I love you."

Emily pulled away from the glass, and Danny pressed closer to it, trying to come through without knowing how. Emily pushed away the desire to go back to the glass and stay there. She couldn't stay. She couldn't remain there and mourn, not because she didn't have time, but because she didn't have the strength. Emily took off her shirt and wrapped it tightly around one hand. It took a few tries because she'd never felt so weak, but she busted the window over the kitchen sink, which clattered loudly around the drain and splashed glass across the floor. She put her shirt on again, little shards cutting her arms and abdomen; then she crawled inside.

And like she'd always done when Em was crying, Danny reached for her with open arms. Emily watched Danny drift away from the door, her friend's unsteady footsteps over the glass covered floor. Emily pulled the gun from her waistband, it took every ounce of her strength, and she was forced to go inside herself to look for more as she looked down the barrel and leveled the sights at Danny's head. "I'm sorry I forgot you. I never will again, and I promise, you'll be all right."

Emily closed her eyes and fired. Danny fell away without goodbye. Outside, Red whined, and scratched at the patio door. He was afraid for her, she thought, but there was nothing left to be afraid of. The worst of it was over. The bad part was gone, and there was only Danny left, the Danny she remembered from the fleeting scenes inside her head. Emily stretched Danny out onto her back, closed her friend's bloodshot eyes, and laid her arms across her stomach to hide the gouge and bone.

She unlocked the patio door and slid it open enough to let Red in. He burst in on alert, and she allowed him to sniff Danny for a moment, until he seemed aware the danger had passed. Emily had nothing left. She didn't sit so much as collapse down beside Danny. Emily pulled her knees to her chest, and hugged them with both arms, the gun still gripped tightly in one hand. Red tolerated this, and for a while sat patiently waiting, but he soon began to pace across the threshold of the door.

She couldn't help but wonder how many friends Red had lost that he could move on so quickly. It was a barbaric skill to learn, and Emily doubted she'd ever be such a master of it. "I know Red. I want to go home too. But we can't." He whined gloomily. "I can't just leave her."

Red sat down with a huff by the patio door and watched the weeds sway in the yard. He wasn't happy about it, but she thought he was giving her leave to do whatever she needed to do. Emily walked around the house as though she'd been there a thousand times. She supposed that was probably true, even though she couldn't remember exactly. She had a sense of where to find everything she needed. Something deep in her still knew, even if the rest had forgotten. In the master bedroom, she found some nice things in Danny's closet. Danny had always had a thing for black shirts, so much that most of the closet was black, which had seemed a little boring before, but was appropriate, considering how things had ended. Emily picked out one that was silky and had little drapes at the elbows like wings, a pair of nice black pants, and one of the hundreds of pairs of glittery-heeled shoes. In a dresser drawer, Emily found a large quilt that looked hand made. All these things she carted to the dining room table, along with hairbrushes and make up, and gauze she found in the medicine cabinet in the bathroom.

Though Danny wasn't a particularly large person, Emily struggled to pull off the vile nightgown. Then she cleaned the wound on Danny's ribs with a bottle of water she found under the sink and covered the area with tape and gauze, so Danny almost seemed whole again. Emily put Danny's body in the clothes, and though it took nearly an hour, she managed to smooth the massive knot in Danny's hair. Emily added a little make up, just enough to dim down the look of Danny's veins, and brighten her face from the miserable grey. Danny had never been one to wear much in the way of makeup. She had a kind of natural beauty, and that was all Emily wanted, for her to look natural again.

She petted Danny's forehead for a few minutes and tried to memorize her face again. It was easy because she hadn't really forgotten, she'd just refused to remember. Then she kissed Danny's forehead, rolled her gently up inside the quilt, and dragged the quilt into the back yard. Emily wished the yard was beautiful. If she thought she could manage Danny's body, she might have carted her to the SUV and taken Danny to rest in her lovely garden, but without help, and with the street so crowded, there was no way.

Emily found a shovel in a small tool shed beside the house. With great care, she pruned back the weeds and thrust the shovel into the dirt. She slammed her foot down to drive it deep, then threw the dirt into a pile. Digging was cathartic, familiar. This much, she had done before.

12

They didn't enjoy the ride home. Even though she rolled the window down, Red didn't want to stick his head outside. Instead, Red sat quietly in the seat, but he looked over at her every now and then. She probably looked like something he'd seen at the garbage dump. Her clothes were filthy, her hands and face were brown with dirt, her nails were crusted with dried black, her hair was wild, and her eyes were nearly swollen closed.

Even when they walked through the front door, Emily couldn't have said she was happy to be home. She looked upstairs at the long path to the shower and thought of drowning herself in scalding water, but she didn't think she could wash off what really mattered, and instead, she wandered into the living room to sit on the sofa and stare out into the back garden at the colors and leaves. It was a faraway peace. She knew it existed, but she didn't have the will or the energy to reach even as far as the backyard.

When the time came to start dinner, it was an act of sheer will that she managed to wash her hands and create something edible. Even that, she did in a haze. It was like watching someone else's hands break beans and slice tomatoes. There was a stranger in her body, moving her arms and feet. She didn't bother making something for herself, and she thought it likely that she'd never really feel like eating again. She set a plate down on the floor for Red, wondering absently if Todd would stay true to his word and bring dog food.

She left a plate for Todd on the counter and went back to the sofa, where the imprint of herself was still outlined in dirt and dead grass. Like a ghost, she drifted back into the hole as if she'd never left. She disturbed nothing and was nothing. Red laid down beside her after he cleaned his plate; his eyes were intense and his expression sympathetic. While she was constantly shifting between the need to feel connected to some living thing, and the need to curl into herself, she could, in neither case, bring herself to pet him. He was content to lay next to her and be her friend; she was grateful he had no other need.

She stared at the garden and thought of Danny. The memories were precious because there were so few, but each of them was as vivid as the daylight on her garden. Sometimes she'd be flooded with something new, a look or a feeling. She wanted to feel it all and to feel completely empty. She tried to focus on all those plants she'd raised to life, but she found herself picking dead grass from her jeans and shredding it to tiny pieces with her fingertips instead. The dead grass felt real, maybe especially because it was dead, and if she could destroy it, she must be real as well.

She wasn't sure how much time had passed between finishing dinner and Todd coming home, but his food was probably cold. When Todd opened the front door, she didn't move, or couldn't. It was hard to be sure. Even when Todd called out to ask her what the dinner was, she didn't answer him. It sounded like he was too far away to care about, like nothing could reach her in that place on the sofa.

It wasn't until he came into the living room and gaped at her with his dinner plate, touched her shoulder and said her name that she momentarily came to life again. He was too close. She brushed his hand away, depressed that she finally felt compelled to speak. "I buried her."

Todd had a knack sometimes for asking stupid questions. "Who?"

She turned her head up to look at him. The room shivered. She felt drunk, but her mouth moved anyway. "Danny. I shot her in the face."

"Jesus. You went wandering off? You could have gotten yourself killed."

Anger, that was familiar. That was real too. No sympathy, no tenderness. He only wanted to call her crazy, as usual. That was okay. Today she was crazy. Maybe tomorrow too. She blinked at him, the shock in her soul ebbing to aggravation. It was a good thing. Nothing was so reanimating as wanting to bash Todd with his own dinner plate. "Did you hear what I said? I shot my best friend in the face, and I cleaned her up, and I buried her."

"I heard you." Todd took a step away. His words were slow and cool.

"And you knew, didn't you? You knew the whole time."

"Emily, Don't. You don't want this."

"How do you know what I want? Why would you lie to me? You remembered everything, my dress, the cake, your brother. You didn't forget my maid of honor. You didn't forget my best friend. I did, and you knew."

Todd swelled with sour outrage. "Of course, I didn't tell you. Look at what it did to you. I didn't tell you because I knew you'd do something crazy, and I was right. You went out to a strange neighborhood and almost killed yourself for no reason."

"No reason?" Emily couldn't get out the rest of what she wanted to say.

Todd interrupted the effort anyway. "There was nothing you could do, Emily."

"Except what I did, but you couldn't let me have that. You wouldn't let me help her."

"And what am I supposed to do if something happens to you. What do you think is going to happen to me?"

She spoke bitterly to the carpet. "You'd have make your own damn dinner."

"Christ, Em. What were you thinking?"

"You wouldn't tell me the truth. What else was I supposed to do?"

Todd returned to his fatherly voice, stiff with logic, oozing with reason. "You're mad at me for trying to protect you, for caring about you enough to not want to upset you. And you ran off where it wasn't safe to punish me for trying to love you. Do you realize how insane that sounds?"

"This isn't about you." She looked down at Red because she couldn't stand to look at Todd anymore. Red was lying patiently on the couch, but his early warning system was sounding the alert. She tried to smooth down his mohawk.

"Yeah, Em. It is. You've been pissed at me forever for no good reason. You act like I'm the worst guy in the world for wanting to protect your feelings. You have no idea how lucky you are to have someone who cares about you that much, so all you ever do is point out everything I do wrong."

"Then stop always doing the wrong thing." Emily pressed her lips together and looked out into the garden again. She wasn't so irrational as to not listen to what he had to say, but none of it rang true. She couldn't feel grateful for him. She couldn't be thankful for a mouth full of lies that had done little more than deny her the opportunity to grieve and heal. She didn't feel lucky at all. She felt sick. She felt dead and hungry. Every time she looked at him all she could see was the lie, and the worst part was how familiar that feeling was. The feeling of mistrusting him, questioning him, was more familiar and more trustworthy than the idea that they ever loved each other at all.

But there was nothing to be done for it. He said he lied to keep her safe, and she understood the reason if not the decision. She didn't want to give him points for doing a shitty thing, but even if she was willing to admit that he tried to do it out of love, it didn't erase the magnitude, the perpetuation of his lie. Emily had to believe if he had kept this from her, this huge, mountain of a thing, there must be other things he kept hidden at the back of the garden shed buried in the dark where the light wouldn't reach.

He made her helpless without the truth. She had no proof that he'd done anything beyond what he'd said, lied to protect her feelings, but she wanted truth more than love, more than anything. "I don't feel lucky. I don't feel grateful. Do you want me to lie to spare your feelings? You must prefer that since it's what you do to me."

"If it meant that I don't have to listen to you criticize everything I do, yeah. Sometimes I'd rather hear you lie through your teeth."

That felt like the most honest thing he'd said to her in weeks. She chewed on the inside of her mouth. "It wasn't always this way."

That was somewhere between a statement and a question, but Todd answered anyway. "No. It wasn't."

"Do you know what changed?"

"No."

She looked at the dog to spare Todd the effort of lying to her face.

13

If Todd wanted her to lie, she would have no guilt in doing it. She had his permission, his damn endorsement never again to tell him the truth about anything. She had no intention of letting him complain. He'd signed the dotted line by his own admission, so she lied. When he woke up that morning, she kissed him on the cheek as though nothing was wrong. She packed him some leftovers in a brown paper sack and drew a little heart on the bag. By the time he left for work, she had him convinced that her sorrow and anger had abated, and they would be as happy as they ever were. But that was the biggest lie. They'd never been happy.

She waited until he was gone and was sure he wasn't going to come home having suddenly forgotten something. Then she cleaned out her backpack and repacked it with necessities. She felt the need, she wasn't sure why, to be extra prepared. She loaded two handguns into the backpack, and another into a holster on her hip, and she took Red, because he was better than her own eyes and pretty good at having her back.

She wasn't certain why she felt the need to

return to the garbage dump. Todd had called her crazy and part of her believed that was true. But Red had seen the man rifling through the garbage bags too. If Todd didn't want her to believe something was real, that was all the motivation she needed to prove that it was. She needed to believe her own eyes. She needed to trust herself beyond all doubt if she couldn't have faith in the only other person she knew.

She headed toward the garbage dump with more than usual trepidation. Traveling through the cones at the construction site made her stomach lurch, and not from looking at the workers, grey and venous in their orange vests. It was more a sick, angry feeling. She stopped the SUV midway through the cones, put the SUV into park, and picked up every single orange cone into a stack by the car. No more blind belief. Those cones were useless. The road would never be finished. The work would never be done. Her questioning the authority of construction zone orange didn't go over well. She pissed off the workers and they walked, herky-jerky toward her, their arms reached out in protest. She was prepared for this. One by one, she hurled the road cones at them with all the strength she possessed. She wasn't particularly good and throwing; her upper body had never been very strong, but the few cones she managed to bop them with were satisfying enough to keep it up, and their startled eyebrows and mouths sagging open in complaint made it a worthy endeavor. When they got close enough for Red to start complaining about them by doing his little dance of discomfort in the seat, she got back in the SUV and left the confused workers standing dumfounded in the center of the pitted road. If they were still there when she came back, she promised herself, she was going to gun it and run them over.

She held her breath as she approached the abandoned garbage truck and those duct taped bags piled around and inside. The bags were probably filled with bones, except the ones festering inside the truck, shielded from bugs and sunlight. There was nothing she could do about that stink and the anger it caused, except to smoosh it away in her guts and let it rot.

She didn't wave to the man in the gatehouse, even after she parked, and he beat the window frantic for her attention. She couldn't think about him or any of those usual things. Today she only wanted to prove to herself that she wasn't crazy. It took a bit of wandering through the mush and stench, but she found the place where she'd first met Red chewing on rotting meat and bones.

Red was not happy to be back in the dump. Though he followed her spryly, he tucked his tail between his legs like he was afraid she might run away and leave him there alone. She petted him often and told him he was a good boy and that she would never, ever leave him. He seemed better with the effort. She climbed the heap, her feet sinking into the morass, and Red climbed beside her where they looked out in the direction where they'd seen the lanky man in the distance. There was no one around. Even Red made no indication that something was wrong, and he'd managed to relax so much that his only interest was to pee on a few things to claim as his own.

She was disappointed. Of course, that didn't mean she hadn't really seen someone out there. No one would want to spend more time at the dump than they had to, and whoever it was might have only been dumping trash like she was. There was no guarantee she'd ever run into him again, but she thought it was at least worth the effort to try.

When she was sure the place was deserted, she wandered further into the dump than she'd ever been before. Deeper in, there weren't as many duct taped garbage bags, but everything was more decomposed. Red found a nest of rats to harass and huge numbers of pigeons pecked the garbage mostly unperturbed at Emily's presence. At first, she found nothing to suggest anyone had been milling through the garbage but her, and she was on the point of giving up and going back. There was only so long someone could tolerate that smell, and rather than becoming used to it, she only felt progressively more lightheaded.

But by accident, when she turned to leave, she noticed a garbage bag sliced open as if someone had been practicing their skill at autopsy. It wasn't unusual for bags to be ripped open at the dump. Red had ripped quite a few just since they'd arrived, but as Emily bent down to investigate, she was certain that no accident or animal had created cuts so straight and clean. The bag had been sliced open with a knife, and since there were very few knife wielders in the world, Emily had all the proof she could need. She hadn't been crazy. Someone had been here.

Now that she had made a positive discovery, she lost the desire to turn back despite her ever-present gag reflex, and in a small radius around the first dissected bag, she found many others that had received the same treatment. She wondered what they could have been looking for in decaying heaps of garbage and regretted that she might never have the chance to ask. Surely, the possibility of running in to that person again was very remote. She felt elated and disappointed all at once, but at least she hadn't been insane, and there was no way in hell she'd let Todd call her so again.

They started back to the car, but they hadn't made it very far before Red stopped and sniffed the air with one filthy paw lifted questioningly in front of him. Emily froze, and watched as the hair on his back stood up straight. He growled, but softly, and bared his teeth the way she might draw her gun in anticipation for a fight.

She should have immediately sprinted for the car, should have, but she didn't. Maybe it was the man she saw. Maybe it was something worse, a real monster this time. Either way, she wanted to know.

"Show me." She commanded, and Red obeyed, walking cautiously, his shoulders low and ready to spring into action. Not far north of where they'd been, she at last saw what made Red so angry. There were three of them. Two large men, one wearing basketball shorts, and the other a rumpled tie, and a woman in a tattered green maxi-dress soaked from the hem to her knees in gore and garbage.

Red sent her a quick look, his feet pressing the ground in turn ready to spring. But she shook her head no. They had no reason to engage. She and Red hadn't been seen, and all the people's backs were turned as if they were transfixed on something else in the garbage heap. It was better just to let them be. But for the first time, Red did not agree. He unleashed a vicious bark and growled, and the three began to turn with interest to the spies that watched them.

"No, Red." Emily shouted and tried to jerk his collar. "Run."

Red was firm; he even pulled her closer.

And she heard the voice cry "help," a voice strained and terrified. At the same time, Red began to charge at the garbage heap three. There was nothing else to do, no more time to think. She bolted after Red and reached the first man as the dog soared up, mouth open, to clamp savagely down on the woman's neck.

Emily drew the gun from her holster and aimed as she moved, and she would have taken him out at the eye if she hadn't slipped in something wet. The shot went through his messy hair and only grazed his skull. But she recovered her footing quickly, and he'd moved so much closer there was practically no need to aim. This time she caught him just above the bridge of his nose, and the shot came out the top of his head because she was so much shorter. He fell to the bottom of the heap, and she turned the barrel at the second man, who was looming toward Red as he ravaged the woman's neck. She wasn't moving, but Red hadn't let her be. Emily would have to talk to him about the overkill. It was going to get the better of him someday.

She caught the second man above his ear, and he fell backwards. His body made a sick squish as he sank into the trash and tumbled down the heap out of sight.

"Red." Red didn't hear her, and he didn't stop. "Red!"

The dog backed away, staring between Emily and the woman he'd killed. Just to make sure, to make him feel better, she put the barrel against the woman's head and pulled the trigger. Red's mouth was dripping black and there was grey flesh caught in his teeth and chunks of it in the fur around his face. "Good boy," she cooed. "Good baby."

"Hello?" That voice again.

She'd almost forgotten why they'd bothered clearing out the area at all. "Hello." She said to the rancid air.

His voice was a little dry and gravelly. "You just saved my life, I think."

"You're welcome, I think."

14

"I hate to admit it, but I think I still need help."

Emily followed the sound of his voice and peered down into the hole in the rubbish where the man she'd killed had fallen. That man, still missing part of the top of his skull, was sprawled on top of another, much smaller, much thinner man with a mess of black hair and narrow eyes.

"I was worried you were a figment of my imagination." Even as she said it, she half expected him to disappear.

"Uh. No. Just a guy, suffocating under another guy."

"Oh yeah. Sorry. Hang on." Emily put the gun back in the holster on her hip. "Stay here and keep watch." She scratched Red behind the ears and he started patrolling. Emily tried to carefully scale down to the man. She was usually pretty light on her feet, but it didn't go well. The trash was loose and wet, and she slid down the last half of the slope, slicing open the side of one leg on a piece of rusty rebar that was poking out from the rest of the garbage. It hurt, and blood quickly mingled with the grossness in her sock. There were more important things. She was able to help just enough to roll the body off of the man beneath.

"Hello." She said again.

"Hi." He sat up and stared at her. His eyes were fierce but kind.

"Why are you in a hole?" Emily squatted down next to him.

"I didn't mean to be. I fell." He blinked and rubbed the back of his head with one dirty hand. "I'd probably be dead if you hadn't found me."

"Why didn't you just run away?"

"Wrenched my ankle. Not even sure I can stand on it, and I lost my gun." He lifted his hands helplessly. "Somewhere in all this trash."

"That was stupid."

"Uh. Yeah. When my life flashed before my eyes, the last thing I saw was how stupid that was. It wasn't a really swell ending." He stuck out a dirty hand for her to shake. "I'm Adam."

"Emily." She took his hand and shook it. "Do you need me to help you up?"

Adam nodded. "Yes, but also, do you have a car?"

"Yeah."

"You're bleeding." Adam frowned and leaned in to look at her leg. "That cut looks pretty bad. What did you snag on?" But his eyes answered his question for him as he looked up the slope. "When's the last time you had a tetanus shot?"

"I don't remember." She touched the skin around the wound. "It hurts a little."

"Shit." Adam put both hands on the back of his head and dragged them around to his face. "This is my fault."

"Yes." She wondered if he was always so prone to state the obvious.

"Look, I can barely walk, and I biked in here."

Emily lifted an eyebrow. "Like an actual bike? With pedals and everything?"

"Yeah." He shook his head. "What else would I mean?"

"I don't know. I thought only little kids rode those or people that did marathons."

"Well no. People use them for other things. They don't need gas."

Emily picked off a piece of plastic that had become tangled in her shoelace. "You don't have to be defensive. I'm glad you ride a bike. I know I'm not imaging anything."

"What does that have to do with me riding a bike?"

"I don't think I'd imagine that sort of thing."

He stared at her the way Todd did sometimes, like she was a zoo monkey. "If you were imagining this, I'd probably be better looking."

"You'd smell better."

"You're kind of weird, Emily."

She watched as another glob of blood ran down her leg to her sock. "As compared to what? All the other girls you've met in a garbage dump?"

"I've never met any other girls here."

"Then, I'm not weird. I'm unique."

Adam laughed, though she hadn't really intended to be funny. "Look, if you help me out of this hole and take me home, I can have a doctor look at that leg and make sure you don't get lock jaw or something. You might need stitches, and God knows what else got in there from all this garbage, and I sort of owe you for saving my ass and all."

"Where do you live?" She wasn't keen on the idea of giving a trash covered stranger a ride home, but she didn't like the idea of leaving him there either, unarmed, and unable to walk.

"Out at the plant."

She cocked her head to the side a bit. "The power plant?"

"Yeah. Me and some others."

"Others?" There was danger in that word. If there were others, she'd be outnumbered, and Todd wouldn't know where to find her if she didn't come home. But there were *others*, and it was as magnetic as it was repulsive. She shook her head forcefully. "I can't do it. I can't pick up some strange man at the dump. What if you decide to kill me?"

"I mean, I'm sorry we didn't meet for coffee or something first, but it is what it is. I need a lift, and you need stitches."

"But other people?"

"It's not a bad crowd. No one will hurt you."

The look of sincerity on his face was so foreign it made her uncomfortable. "How many others?"

"Near five hundred now, I think."

Emily fell back out of her squat and landed hard on her butt. "Jesus."

He drew his eyebrows close. "How long have you been on your own?"

"What? I'm not on my own." The words rushed out of her. "I'm married, and my husband would kill me."

"Well it's not a date. It's a car ride. You don't think he'd do the same thing?"

"He's kind of an asshole, but this time he'd be right. It isn't safe. Five hundred people? Really?"

"I just saw that dog of yours almost take a head off. No one is going to hurt you."

She looked up. Red was staring down into the hole expectantly. "He's a good boy. I picked him up here at the dump a few days ago. He was eating," Emily frowned, "things that weren't nice."

"Then you've already picked up a stranger

at the dump, and that worked out okay." He looked up at the dog, who even she had to admit was a little terrifying with flesh and gore smeared on his face.

"I guess so." The cut on her leg throbbed and burned. "We should get out of this hole."

Adam nodded, and careful to avoid putting weight on his left foot, he let her help him up. They spent a few minutes looking around in the garbage for his gun, but with no luck and both of them in pain, they didn't put much effort into it.

"It's a shame," he said wiping his hands on his pants. "I really liked that gun."

"I'm deeply sorry for your loss."

Climbing up the garbage slope was slow and difficult with only two uninjured legs between them. They slipped down again once, but on the second try, after taking the path a few inches at a time, they managed to climb up to where Red was waiting on them. Red circled Adam with a leery series of snorts and sniffs, but Adam passed examination. Red seemed to think he was safe enough. Red followed them to the car, weaving behind them, keeping a lookout, and occasionally darting forward to study them both with concern.

By the time Emily got back to the car and was able to put some pressure on her cut, she was beginning to think that it might not be so bad to see a professional. After all, she was always telling Mr. Johnson not to be so stubborn about the cut on his hand, and she'd hardly be setting a good example if she let her leg fall off from some gross garbage dump infection.

She wiped her leg with a questionable towel she'd found in the back seat, then covered the passenger seat with an emergency blanket. "No offense." She said to him as she shooed him slightly out of the way. "But you really stink."

"I'm so gross, I disgust myself." He climbed in on top of the emergency blanket, and she opened the back door for Red to jump in. He seemed slightly perturbed that Adam got the front but finally settled down and stretched himself out across the back seat.

She was already feeling like she'd made a mistake helping Adam, if for no other reason than the awkwardness. She tried to make conversation, even though it might have been the smarter thing to just ask for directions and let the silence alone. "Why the power plant?"

He shrugged and looked out the window. "It's far enough out of town not to get much traffic. It's got a lot of walls with no windows. It's got power."

"That's smart, I guess."

"It wasn't my idea. The others found and let me in. When everything happened, a few of the power plant employees who didn't have kids or families nearby stayed to try and keep the place on as long as they could. It was like, company policy that they had to have all these survival supplies in case of war or natural disasters and stuff."

"So, you all just sort of sit around at the power plant?"

Adam laughed. "I wish. That'd be nice. We all have jobs. It takes all of us to keep that place functioning."

"What is your job?"

"I'm usually a runner."

She glanced at him with half a smile. "It doesn't seem like you're very good at it."

He laughed. "Well not right now. But usually."

"What do you run for?"

"Supplies mostly. Scavenge. Whatever we need. The dump is a good place to find some things if you know what you're looking for."

"So, you didn't actually work at the plant?"

He lifted an eyebrow at her. "The actual plant is shut down mostly. After it happened, when it wasn't practical to keep the place running anymore, the guys that worked there shut it all down. If they hadn't, it would have been a disaster for the whole city. You never wondered why you didn't melt or go up in smoke?"

The idea that the power plant even existed had been so far removed from her mind she could barely mumble a response. "I have solar."

He chewed on his lip. "Okay."

She did not like the way he looked at her at all. The sooner she could be rid of him the better. She tried to remind herself of why she'd come in the first place, just to prove he was real; she never thought that there could be too much real, but he somehow managed it with every blink of incredulity.

She'd never had so much trouble talking before. Her mouth didn't want to form words, and her brain didn't want to provide her mouth with words to form. "My husband used to work for SolarStar before they closed. He installed and repaired solar panels. But they closed because of the recession, and now he manages the hardware store."

"He manages a-," Adam cleared his throat. "Knowing how to install solar. Yeah. I could see how that would be a useful skill to have nowadays. I was a mechanic. I used to work at a shop that built high end custom cars for rich people with too much money. Not much use for that anymore. I still work on the cars sometimes though. I still like doing it."

"I see." She shifted uncomfortably in the driver's seat and put the keys in the ignition. From the back seat, Red was breathing down her neck and his breath was exceptionally bad.

"How about you? What did you do before?"

She frowned. "I don't understand. Before what?

Adam stared at her with what looked like stifled curiosity, one eyebrow lifted, nose slightly scrunched, and an awkward smile. "So, you're a housewife?"

"What? No. That's not what I mean."

He was giving her that annoying look again. "You've never had a job?"

She shot him an impatient look. "Of course, I have."

"Then what did you do?"

"I-" But she couldn't remember. Whatever the answer to that question was, it was lost in the black space and out of reach. "It's none of your business. Stop asking me questions."

He held up his hands. "I'm sorry. I was just making conversation. We don't have to talk if you don't want to."

She frowned. "I'm sorry. I didn't mean to bark at you. I grow things. I think I have always liked to grow things. Maybe that was, that is my job." She gripped the wheel tighter and tried to avoid his gaze. "Sometimes I forget. . . I think I don't remember how to talk to people anymore that answer back."

15

Adam didn't say much after that except to give directions, and she was grateful. She didn't understand herself. She got so mad at Todd for not telling her the truth, but now that she'd found out that Adam was real, that there were a lot of very real people in the world, a big part of her wished she hadn't figured that out. The world looked different, even the grass and trees had shifted their shades of green with the knowledge that she wasn't alone. She'd felt that there were people enough to talk to. Even Mr. Johnson wasn't terrible company, but now even the thought of his naked conversation made her apprehensive. Five hundred others. It should have been a good thing, but it didn't feel good. It felt terrifying.

Adam told her to turn on to a dirt road at the edge of town, and they headed into the low hills. She stared ahead, trying not to look at him.

It was hard enough to hear him on the few occasions where he told her where to go, let alone see him too. Fortunately, the drive wasn't long. After about 20 minutes, they approached a wooden guard tower that looked newly built.

Adam took a flashlight from his pocket and turned it on and off three times. Then he waited and turned it on and off again. It was some kind of signal, she guessed, to let the people in the tower know that they were friends. She felt the tension of fear spread throughout her arms and back, but nothing happened as they passed the tower.

A few minutes later, they were at another guard shack, and a huge chain link fence that stretched as far in either direction as the hills would let her see. Behind the fence, there were more guard towers peering over the hoops of barbed wire at the top. She could see the now useless concrete towers of the plant twisting into the sky. But none of this bothered her, it was architecture, and there was nothing scary about wood and stone; it was the people. Two perched on each tower with black rifles and scopes.

The guard in the booth was in full body armor, only his face exposed between his helmet and his collar. He had a black mustache and goatee and looked like he'd been wrapped in Kevlar as a baby. She felt her hands shaking on the wheel as she pulled slowly up to the shack and rolled down her window as Adam instructed. She stared straight ahead, afraid to move, or breathe as Adam said a few words to the guard and laughed about how stupid he'd been.

The guard waved them through, and the car crawled forward and climbed onto the pavement. But she could barely see. She felt her eyes trying to roll back in her head. She gripped the wheel tight enough for her hands to hurt but it still didn't stop them from shaking. She wanted to go home. She didn't want to be here and. . .

She heard a woman scream. And guns, the chorus of automatic fire. Shouting, moaning, and snapping teeth.

"Emily?" Adam grabbed the wheel, but she couldn't answer. She knew he was beside her in the car, that they were safe, that nothing was wrong, but she could smell something burning. No. Not something. Everything. Everything was on fire, and she had to run. She had to find Todd, she had to. . .

"Emily!" That time Adam screamed it. She felt a hand close on her wrist, and her eyes swam to it through smoke and shrill cries. She stared at his fingers, long and thin, pink flesh, warm. "Are you ok?"

She saw Adam but couldn't move. Somehow, she formed words. "I want to go home."

"Emily, there's nothing to be afraid of. I'm not going to hurt you. No one is going to hurt you. Do you believe me?"

She looked into his eyes and found honesty easily, mostly because it was an unfamiliar thing. She nodded.

"Breathe." Adam looked straight into her.

And it was only then she realized that her lungs were burning, and she was holding her breath. She gasped and went in to such a hacking cough from the sudden dryness of the air on her throat that she nearly vomited. They'd come to a stop, which was lucky. She hadn't even noticed pushing down the break.

"What's wrong?" Adam tried to take hold of her hand, but she jerked it away.

"I feel like I'm dying. I heard someone scream."

"No one is screaming. Everything is fine." Adam's face did not reflect anything that looked like fine. He looked more afraid than she felt, but it was a fear for her and not for himself. "Let's just get you in to see the doctor, and then you can go home, if that's what you want."

He told her where to turn and where to park, and when she killed the engine, she felt relieved of at least one thing less to have to think about. The building in front of them looked as if it had once been an office, but the windows were covered in bars and chain link. That much was not in the design of the original architect. There was a metal sign nailed up beside the door.

"Human resources?"

"We thought it was funny."

The door was locked, and they had to wait to be let inside. Adam explained that it was part of their policy to lock doors all the time. It helped to keep an infection from spreading because everyone inside was quarantined, just in case. A small woman with short black hair, wearing jeans and a purple t-shirt, answered the door. She smiled when she first saw them, but her face cooled quickly to professionalism when she saw them both limp inside. "Sit down. Both of you."

They sat in black leather chairs with metal frames, and Emily realized they were in some kind of small lobby. There was still a desk built in to the floor, but there was nothing on it. "Who's this and what did you do now?" The doctor pulled Emily's foot up onto another chair.

"Barbara, this is Emily, and she just saved my life."

Barbara squatted down to get a better look at Emily's leg. Red scooted out of the way to give her some room. "Lost some skin doing it I see. She's going to need stitches."

"I thought, but she got cut on this rusty rebar, and she can't remember the last time she had a tetanus shot."

Barbara nodded. "Well, we've got them." Barbara smiled at Emily. "Lucky you."

Adam looked at the floor. "Not as lucky as me, though. I thought I was gone for sure."

Barbara looked at him accusingly. "And what did you do?"

"Well I'm hoping you're going to tell me I sprained an ankle and didn't break anything."

"I'll tell you whatever you want, but it might not be true. You're going to have to wait though. She's worse off than you." She turned to look at Red as he laid down on the floor. "And is there anything wrong with you?"

Red wagged his tail and laid his head down on his paws.

"Nothing a bath won't cure, huh? At least one of you is okay. Wait here. I'll get some things ready. Put those legs up. Don't make them worse by letting them dangle. Try not to drip on the floor."

But Adam stood up instead of doing what she ordered. "I'm feeling better, Barbara. Let me come help you."

Barbara opened her mouth, seemingly to scold him, but closed it again after a slight nod of Adam's head, and she gestured for him to walk first down the hallway to their left. Emily could hear Adam's unsteady footfalls drifting up the hall.

Emily didn't keep her foot up and instead bent down to pet Red. He was more comforting to her than anything in that place, no matter how much medicine they kept inside. "I'm sorry, baby. We'll be home soon. We shouldn't have come here. We shouldn't have wanted to know." Red lifted his head to yawn and then laid it down again, content to be scratched and coddled after their busy day.

Adam and Barbara were gone for what seemed like at least ten minutes, and during that time, Emily thought of getting up, running for the car, and speeding out of that place as quickly as she could. Only the throbbing in her leg stopped her. When they came back, they both wore the kind of cheerful looks that Emily associated with people heavy with bad news.

"Come with me. We'll get you up on a bed in the light, so I can see what you need." Barbara offered Emily a hand getting up, which Emily accepted reluctantly. Sitting still had increased the pain, but she tried very hard not to limp.

Red tried to follow her, but Barbara bent down to scratch between his shoulders. "Not you, honey. You're not clean. You stay here, and I'll get your mommy back to you in a minute." Red sat down again and let his tongue lop out the side of his mouth.

Red seemed to trust Barbara even easier than he'd trusted Adam. That much at least eased some of the anxiety Emily felt. Emily followed Barbara to the first door down the hall, which, though clearly not its original purpose, had been set up like any doctor's office should be. Barbara offered her a cloth gown to wear while she looked at the leg, but Emily told her just to cut off the jeans. "I got a new pair. They have butt butterflies. I don't really need these."

Barbara nodded, and Adam flopped down

in a chair in the corner. Barbara cut off Emily's pant leg with a pair of surgical scissors and began to clean the wound with cotton balls and peroxide. Emily bit the side of her cheek to avoid squirming at the sting. "Adam tells me you're married."

Emily nodded.

"Me too. 27 years now. We're lucky to have made it together."

"Sure." Emily winced as Barbara pulled a small piece of metal from the wound with a pair of tweezers. "Anybody's lucky to make it these days. So many people get divorced. I'm pretty sure there's some people on my block having an affair."

Barbara shot Adam a quick look Emily couldn't comprehend but somehow still found incredibly rude. "Are you allergic to anything, Emily?"

"What?"

"You know, food, antibiotics? You're probably going to need something for this, so it won't get infected. I don't want to give you something that might make you sick."

"I don't-" Emily chewed on her lip hard enough that she could taste copper in her mouth. "I don't remember."

"You ever had surgery?"

Barbara's voice was very kind, but even the kindness made Emily feel angry. "I don't remember."

"Well, what about injuries? A concussion,

anything like that?"

"Todd said something happened to my head. I don't remember. That was months ago, and it doesn't matter now." She turned dourly to look at the wall.

"How about medication? Have you been on anything?"

Emily nodded. "Birth control, and sometimes Tylenol, when Todd gives me a headache."

"My husband gives me headaches too. Worth it though. Never Penicillin? Anything a doctor gave you besides the BC?"

Emily shook her head angrily. "Stop asking me questions."

"Okay. Okay. Everything is all right. Lay back there and let me stitch you up, and you can be on your way."

Emily's heart thumped and even she didn't understand why this was making her feel so pissed off. They'd both been kind, and all she could do was writhe inside and want to scream at them. She tried to breathe, to stare at the lights on the ceiling, and not to think.

"Adam says you thought you heard someone scream."

Emily growled. "Because I heard someone scream."

"Is that," Barbara cleared her throat, "is that the first time that's happened?"

Emily could feel her shoulders shuddering with the restraint it took to keep from shouting. "What do you mean?"

Barbara sat back while she prepared the needle and surgical thread. "Well, it sounds to me like maybe you had a panic attack."

Emily rolled her eyes so hard her whole head moved. "I don't have panic attacks."

"Okay. Hold still now. This will hurt a little." Emily clenched her fists as Barbara put five stitches in her calf and tied them off.

"All better. Sit up now. We'll get you your shot, and you can go as you please."

Emily looked at Adam in the corner. He was staring at her with his eyes in such stiff concentration he seemed to scowl, but he wasn't angry. He was concerned, almost tender.

Emily clenched her fists again. "Sometimes. . ." She hesitated.

Barbara smiled. "Sometimes what?"

"Sometimes, I get these memories. Sometimes I dream."

"That happens to all of us. It's okay that it happens to you too." Barbara was trying to sound very comforting, but the effort echoing in her voice had quite the opposite effect.

Adam sat up rigidly in the chair. "What kind of memories?"

"I remembered a girl I knew. I'd forgotten. Her name was Danny. Todd thought I was crazy, but I wasn't. She was a person. I found her. I buried her."

"That was kind of you, Emily. Give me your arm now. A little pinch. This will be sore tomorrow, but it shouldn't be too bad. If it gets bad, if it hurts too much or swells up more than you think it should, you come back and see me."

Emily wiped her eyes and chewed her lip again. "Todd wouldn't like it if I came back. Can I go now?"

"Sure." Barbara said taking off her gloves. "Feel better, okay?"

Adam shot Barbara a look of irritation. "Wait." He stood up too quickly, put too much weight on his ankle, and ended up falling back into the chair. "You came all this way. Let me show you around at least."

"I don't know if that's a good idea." Barbara frowned and amended herself. "Both of you should keep off your feet."

"I'll take the golf cart. I think maybe she should see."

Emily twisted her hands together. "I don't want to see anything. I want to go home."

"We've got a pool table, and an espresso machine," Barbara offered.

Emily shook her head.

"What about the garden?" Adam tried standing up again, this time more slowly. "You said you grow things. We grow things too."

"You have a garden?"

"Well not me personally. I could kill a house plant just by looking at it, but there's one here. Lots of people take care of it and use what they need."

Barbara smiled at Adam. "We've managed to get quite a collection growing."

"I'll look." Emily said guardedly. "As long as I can take Red."

"Sure. He can pee on everything."

Emily sort of laughed. Red would not wait for permission to pee on anything, but it was good that she didn't have to worry about it.

"First, that foot. Your turn." Barbara patted the table, and Adam and Emily switched places.

It didn't take Barbara long to figure out that Adam had a bad sprain and needed to take it easy for a few days. She told him to keep ice on it whenever he could, gave him some anti-inflammatory medicine, and wrapped his ankle in an ace bandage. Then she gave Emily some pills to keep infection at bay.

Barbara shook Emily's hand like they were at a real doctor's office somewhere in the city. "Take care, Emily. I hope you'll come back and see me if. . . well if you need anything."

"Okay." She didn't know what else she was supposed to say. "Thanks."

Adam led Emily and Red out a side door where a golf cart was sitting with the keys in the ignition. Emily climbed into the front seat and Red jumped into the back and prepared to feel the cool wind in his ears, though she feared the ride would not quite live up to his canine expectations. They pulled around the corner of the building and Adam pointed out things as they passed. There was a huge field of solar panels, which he told her had been installed as a way to diversify the plant's power production before it closed. She wondered if Todd had installed any of them but couldn't remember him mentioning working at a plant. There were people milling about. Inside, away from the towers and the guns, the people seemed quite normal. Occasionally, Adam would stop and introduce her to someone which was about as comfortable as setting her on fire. She was glad for Red again, because he was a furry shield between her and the others. Red was social where she felt only awkwardness. The fact that Red's face was covered in gore made little difference to his charisma, but Emily shrank away and only tried for some of a smile while the rest of her worried about reeking of garbage and not knowing what to say.

By the time they reached the plant's garden, she was more tired than she ever remembered being. She told herself it was the loss of blood, but after so much anger at Todd for lying, she couldn't believe her own lies. It was being around the others that made her feel this way, drained and slow. Even listening to people's conversation was exhausting.

At first glance, the garden seemed worth the effort. It was huge, at least ten times bigger than her own, and they were using fresher fertilizer. Todd explained they had livestock, a small herd of cattle, chickens, pigs, rabbits, even a few horses. He liked the rabbits, especially, he said, and couldn't eat them on principle because they were adorable. Emily wandered through fragrant herbs and stopped to breathe in the mint and rosemary. Adam noticed the attention she lavished on these two. "You can take some home with you if you like. We won't miss it."

"No." Emily said firmly. She'd already accepted more of their help than she preferred. "I just like the smell is all, it makes me think."

Adam leaned in for a snoot full of basil. "About what?"

"I don't know." She thought she sounded distant, or high, or both.

He laughed. His front two teeth were kind of crooked. "Do you often think about what you don't know?"

She scowled at him. "Yeah. Sometimes." She grunted with frustration. "It just makes me think. It's like a farm almost."

"Yeah, minus that special brand of garbage stink we're adding to the mix."

"No, even the garbage. We used to

compost. There was always a pile of rotting garbage and pig crap behind the sty, but when the wind would blow. . ." Emily felt her knees turn into pudding, and she saw with too much clarity the image of her childhood home, rows of wheat for what seemed like eternity, her house, small and white with yellow shutters on the windows, and her father in his overalls slinging hay bales onto a truck bed. Her mother in jeans and a sweatshirt, dumping a bucket into the troth for the hogs and calling them to come and eat. It was painful to think of, but she didn't want to stop. She could have shut down right then, stayed in that space in her brain until she died.

"You grew up on a farm?" Adam's face was at once curious and disinterested.

She could only assume that a blend of those two things required some deliberate effort on his part. "I want to go home."

"Sure. I'll drive you back to your car."

"No. That's not what I mean. I want to go home to the place I'm thinking of."

Adam shifted uncomfortably, keeping off his ankle. "I'd drive you there, if I could."

She felt a tear slip down her face and turned from him to brush it away. He wasn't as stupid as Todd. He knew to stay silent.

She didn't have anything else to say to him and was grateful when he didn't ask her any more questions. The drive back to the car was a blur of colors and voices. When they got back, Adam told Red goodbye and thanked them both again for saving his life.

Emily didn't tell him she wished she had never gone to the dump that day, that she was glad he was alive but sorry for it all at the same time. She felt that place had lit a fuse inside that was burning slowly, and she had no idea how many explosives were waiting in her soul at the other end.

Adam told her to come back anytime.

16

She didn't know how long Todd's dinner sat on the counter getting cold before he opened the front door. She wasn't sure if she remembered to wash her hands before she made it or if he was going to eat half a garbage dump. She wasn't sure how long she sat on the sofa, letting the stink permeate while she stared out the patio door into the garden. She was wandering through a farm in her brain, finding her way into familiar corners and secret places she had known since she was a little girl. She knew Red followed her everywhere, yellow fur still stained, and he let her stroke him for what seemed like five minutes or forever or both. He was the only thing she let in from the present. The only thing worth keeping.

She didn't look up when Todd came into the room, and she knew it was because he was the last face in the world she wanted to see. Even the thought of Mr. Johnson's shriveled member flopping around on a stripper pole would be easier than having to spend five minutes in Todd's company. She wanted to go home, but the place they lived would never be home, no matter how much she decorated, no matter how much she swept and dusted and cleaned.

And yet she'd made him dinner, like a drone hovering on autopilot around the kitchen. That had to mean something, but she wasn't sure what. She heard him call to her from the kitchen, but she didn't answer. She heard the plate slide off the counter, and the silverware drawer open, but she couldn't bring herself to move. She was afraid, if she twitched so much as a muscle, she would run away and keep running until there was no place left to run.

She heard him come into the living room, and she could feel his eyes digging a mineshaft into her. She couldn't blame him. She couldn't imagine how she and Red looked, disheveled, filthy, covered in blood. She wished she'd showered. She wished a lot of things.

She didn't know how long he stood there staring at her because all she had to measure the passage of time was a light breeze outside shivering the leaves. Finally, Todd walked across the living room floor like he was afraid the sound of a footstep might echo and break her, and then he sat down on the couch and turned on the TV. "What's for dinner, baby?"

Why did people insist on asking her so many questions? How could he pretend that everything was okay? He always asked her, and she always had to think of something. But not today. Today, nothing. She could think of nothing.

"Em, what did you make?"

She blinked.

"Sweetheart." His voice had the kind of command her brain found irresistible, but she tried.

Her body fought itself not to turn, and the motion felt like pulling bags of sand through the mud. "What?"

"What did you cook for dinner, Em? It looks really good."

Nothing. He was going to say nothing. Here she was, looking like she'd scrambled through hell and feeling like she'd just watched the world burn, and he was going to pretend it wasn't real, like nothing happened. She wanted to hurt him, to throw something at him, to claw his eyes out or bash his head in, but all she could do was watch the wind and shiver. She wished she could pretend he wasn't real, the way he pretended. "It's coyote, Todd."

"Em?"

"Every day, the same fucking question. It's coyote. It's always been coyote. It always will be coyote. There's nothing else. You bring it home wrapped in plastic with a sticker like you just went down to the supermarket and put it in a cart. But there are no supermarkets. There's just coyote. You make me pretend every day that it's something else. Every day I think of something stupid to say and we eat and pretend. I'm tired of eating, and I'm fed up with pretending." The walls around their living room seemed to shudder like a stone in a pond.

"Emily. . ."

"Don't speak." She held up a grimy hand that had definitely not been washed. "I saved someone's life today. If I had listened to you, if I'd have let you make me think I was weak and crazy, he'd be dead now. But he's alive because of Red and me, and all you want is to know what I made for dinner, like it doesn't mean anything. You treat me like there's nothing out there, like this house is the center of the planet. But you're not the only person in the world, and neither am I."

"Emily, you can't keep going out this way."

"Why don't you zip tie me to a cash register? There are *others*. So many others. They live. They grow things, but we don't grow, Todd. We only shrink."

Todd scooted toward her with the most ridiculous look on his face, like he was going to try and hold her, or comfort her, or something that would mean nothing like everything else.

"Don't say anything. Don't do anything." She wasn't sure how it happened, but her legs moved, and she stood up from the sofa. She'd been sitting so long the garbage had dried and cracked on her jeans. "I'm tired of remembering."

He didn't listen. He set his plate down, and came swooping at her with his arms out, wanting to know what happened, but he was too late. Too late to ask and too late to try and hold her to keep the world away. It was already inside, even the ugly parts.

She moved for the stairs and Red followed her, cutting Todd off and almost making him stumble. She was half way up the stairs when Red caught up to her heals. She floated past the closed doors in the hall of empty things and locked the bedroom, so Todd couldn't follow her. She heard him banging on the door, begging to be let in, begging to help her, to hold her. She only wanted him to go away. She didn't remember getting in the shower, or scrubbing the dog, and crying because she couldn't lift the horrible red stain. They soaked the sheets together, neither of them really dry and both too exhausted to care. She shuddered on top of the blanket, staring at the ceiling, and the shapes in the plaster that underwent metamorphosis every time she closed her eyes. Emily hoped she didn't dream; she hoped she did.

17

It was almost like she'd gotten her wish. When she opened her eyes, it seemed like she was lodged firmly between her pillow and a dream. Everything was different, just like in dreams that mimic life.

Other than laying there, watching shadows crawl across the ceiling, mimicking life seemed like the best thing to do. She reached for routine like well-worn jeans, comfortable, broken in.

In the mornings, she snuck outside to tend the garden. She crept in the grass and bent to pull the weeds. She did this because it was the way she remembered things to be. Red raced, and slobbered, and peed on things. He was awake, even when she didn't want to be.

There were so many weeds, it was like she hadn't pulled them up in days. But that couldn't be. The garden was every morning, the same thing. Wasn't that how it was supposed to be?

She sat back and watched Red snapping his teeth at a bee, aside from him dancing around, the garden was perfectly at peace. Next door, Mr. Johnson moaned a song she didn't recognize, but she was glad he was having a pleasant enough day to try and sing. Not that she wanted to talk to him, but glad all the same. When the weeds were gone, and the fruits obtained, she opened the garden shed to put some things away. It looked like someone had ransacked the place. She sat down her basket and grunted at herself. This was her fault, this insane disarray.

She stacked up the boxes in the back of the shed where they'd always been, sneaking them as silently as possible into a pile out of the way, but one of the boxes caught the corner of a screwdriver and it clattered into a metal bin on the floor.

Mr. Johnson sighed with glee.

There was no avoiding him now. If she was determined to live in this imitation, then she would do as she had always done. She paused for a deep breath, not feeling much like a morning chat, but she reached for the stepladder all the same. "Good morning, Mr. Johnson." Her voice sounded cartoonish with how much force it took to sound neighborly. She sat the stepladder up near the fence and climbed up to see him face to face.

Mr. Johnson shuffled over in all his half-naked ingloriousness and lifted an arm to wave. Other parts of him always waved. She tried not to make a disgusted face. 'He's dead,' she heard a voice whisper in the back of her brain. "Isn't this weather great? I love it when the seasons start to change."

Mr. Johnson dipped his chin then lifted his face. He'd never struck her as a man to admire much beauty in the world; he was more appreciative of comfort than aesthetic things.

'You're talking to a dead man.' The voice in the back of her head tried to scream. Emily blinked the idea of it away and focused on Mr. Johnson. "Did I tell you we got a dog?"

He made a sound of disapproval deep in his throat, and it made Emily shudder. She'd never been afraid of him before.

Mr. Johnson was her friend, even if she hated admitting it. Emily waved a dismissive hand. "Oh, don't worry. He's a good dog, very sweet, and it's so nice to have the company. You know, I'm over here by myself most days."

Mr. Johnson stretched both arms toward her, a look of sadness, of hunger on his face.

'Hunger?' She thought, and her heart skipped a beat. Why would she think of that?

"I appreciate the gesture, but I can't expect you to keep me company all day. You've got things to do." People to flash. She smiled at him and hoped he couldn't read her mind.

'He is a dead man.'

She wished she could stop reading her own mind. He twisted his neck and clenched his teeth. Emily felt her stomach lurch with disgust and her knees tremble. She couldn't be afraid. It was Mr.

Johnson. Dick. Just like it had always been.

"You're a good friend."

Mr. Johnson's bathrobe got caught on a high weed. He looked at it stuck to the brush with slow and steady befuddlement.

She looked up at the second-floor window with its curtains drawn and its twisting strand of green. "I should let you get on with your day."

Mr. Johnson grunted twice and closed his hands in the air.

"I know. Todd makes me miserable sometimes." She smiled. "But there are worse things he could do." Like never wear pants. "Bye Mr. Johnson. Have a great day."

She could hear him pounding on the wall as she tucked the ladder away. "Come on, Red."

He was a good boy, always a good boy, and he followed her into the family room. Emily looked around and frowned. The sky was only mildly overcast, but she still had to turn on a lamp to see, and it seemed like such a shame. There was a window over the kitchen sink, and a trio of windows along one wall, and even though they only looked out on the cinderblock fence, they would still let in some natural light. The house was so gloomy, so claustrophobic some days. That was normal, she told herself. The darkness was normal.

But she abhorred this normal, always being in the dark. Todd had gone out for a run, which she assumed meant a run down to the convenience store for beer more than it meant a run intended to be healthy in any way. Still, she probably had time to surprise him with a little change. Wasn't change supposed to be normal too? Nothing could stay the same.

She grabbed a crowbar from the garage and approached the painted boards on the windows with determination. She hummed a song; she thought it might have been one the DJ played at her wedding, and she had to be careful not to damage the window frame. Board by board, she let in the light. She'd forgotten how bright, how cheerful it could be, but it seemed like a good morning for remembering.

When the family room was free, she moved on to kitchen, and the formal living room. What was the purpose, she wondered, of cutting off the view of their pretty, perfect street? She stripped off the boards, feeling more weightless with every loose nail. Finally, it seemed like only the stairwell and some little piece of herself was left in darkness.

She stood at the bottom stair, looking up at the door that was always closed, Surely, that window would let in the light, if the door was open, the sun would shine down the stairs and stop the last piece of darkness.

A wave of dizziness. She paused to grip the railing and steady the carpet under her feet. Red followed her, tail whipping, happy to be moving, and she felt better, by small increments. So, she climbed another stair, and another, until she was nearly at the top of the staircase, eyes level with the doorknob she wanted very much to reach and fling open to let in the glorious light.

But the front door slammed open, and she stopped and was forced to turn around on the shadowy stairs. Todd was standing in the open doorway, and he reminded her of a bull stomping the dirt and snorting with flared nostrils and narrow eyes. "What the hell are you doing?"

Her heart sank. She tried so hard to make him happy, but it always turned out this way. She was a child. She sat down on the stairs and wrapped her arms around her knees. "It's always so dark. I just wanted to let in the sun. I thought you'd like it. I thought you'd be happy."

"Emily, we need these." He picked up a board and grimaced at the crooked nail she'd pried from the window frame.

He was so angry; she'd never seen him look so mean. "I'm sorry, Todd." She heard her voice break a little. "I shouldn't have moved your things."

Todd's anger leaked out of him, and in its place a look of perplexity, as if she were some curious thing in a museum of oddities. He leaned a board against the wall and sat down at her feet. "Em, are you okay?"

She nodded and wiped a tear across her face. "Yes. I'm just sad I made you angry. Isn't that the way it is supposed to be? I just wanted to let the sun in. The house is so dark; I just wanted the light to touch me."

He sighed, and she thought it looked less like frustration and more like relief. "Don't cry, Em." His voice had brightened up, like warm rays piercing a cloud. "No harm done. We can hang them up again. You can hand me nails, and I'll hammer things back together."

"I don't want to go back in the dark."

He took her hand and wrapped it in two of his so that it disappeared completely, but he peeled back one hand a little, so he could kiss her fingers. "It's not the low light that makes you unhappy, Em."

She pulled her hands away from him because he was right. It was the death, the unending dark, that no amount of sun could reach.

"Help me fix this, and then we'll be okay, like always."

"Always." She caught a tear before it completely left her eye. "Always somewhere between awake and a dream."

'A nightmare,' said the voice in her brain.

18

They spent the rest of the afternoon undoing the damage she'd done. Every nail was like a little stake into her heart, but Todd was so strangely happy, it made things seem easier, even if they weren't. Slowly, they slipped back into the dark, but it was less lonely, less hollow than it had before seemed. They watched movies, she made dinner, vegetarian lasagna with things from her garden, and when they went to bed, he'd convinced her that all she really needed was a little bit of change.

It made perfect sense really. She did the same thing day after day, disgustingly routine. She supposed that was how marriage was meant to be, finding something that kind of worked and keeping at it until they were too old to remember they'd basically spent their entire lives doing the same stupid things. So instead of heading to the garden for a morning with the tomatoes and undoubtedly a discussion with the perpetually naked Johnson, she decided to go out the front door instead. She packed light, only a small hand gun on her hip. Red trotted beside her, as much ready for a run as she had been. She waved to the little boy that lived at last house on the corner. He was always playing in the yard no matter the time of day, and she wondered about his parents, letting him roam around with no supervision all the time. She waved to the white-haired lady that had nothing better to do than sit on the porch and watch the neighbors go by, and she waved to the man in the shirt and tie who sat in his car and occasionally honked the horn while he waited on his wife and family to come out for the day.

Red had endless joy for exercise. When pausing at the intersections to catch their breath, Red's tongue lolled from his mouth in radiant doggie glee. She started to feel better the harder she breathed, and before too long, she was convinced wholeheartedly that Todd had been right. He was so kind, always looking out for her, so forgiving even when he shouldn't be.

She'd put in earbuds for the run. It had been a long time since she listened to anything but the emptiness of the house, and all the music was new again as the songs shuffled by on random, sometimes slow ballads completely inappropriate for a run. She didn't mind. Every song brought with it little memories, most of them happy, a few that made her soul sing.

Except she heard a song sometimes that made her angry, everything was great. She couldn't remember why some songs made her feel that way, and sometimes she'd see a flash between the pounding of her feet on the sidewalk and the silence between the end of one and the start of another tune.

Sometimes it was fire, tall and wide, smoke filling the sky. She'd blink, and the street was as it had always been. Sometimes it was Danny laughing; she'd shake the sound from her ears and wave to the neighbor shuffling to the mailbox in filthy pajamas.

Sometimes the moments were hot and fast, a scream, a jolt of fear, a farm with fields of wheat that felt like sweet cream and sadness. Sometimes the feeling was vague, a flash of rage, unreasonable emptiness. Sometimes it was specific, the color of a coffee cup, a nose full of mint and rosemary, black veins and eyes painted with red spider webs. Guns firing. That, she heard in every song, every moment, each footstep, and heartbeat.

She felt her feet go heavy and her breath ragged. All those thoughts, and she'd forgotten to think about breathing. At the next broken streetlight, she doubled over, wondering why the hell she'd come so far and thinking that she should have stayed home in the garden after all. But that was the point of it. Breathe. To make her want to stay at home. Breathe. To kill the urge, she had to leave home forever. Breathe. She rubbed her side, which did nothing to stop the cramping there, and forced herself to stand up.

Breathe.

It was then she realized what Red had long since noticed, judging by the height of his mohawk. There was another jogger on the street. Emily forgot to breathe. That was a thing that didn't matter. Air was something she didn't need.

The other woman was wearing a purple sports bra, and her boobs were kind of oozy out the top and woven with thick black veins. She had on black stretch pants and pink running shoes with white laces, ridiculous. She didn't want to run, she wanted to stop traffic with her bright shoes, oozy boobs, her skintight pants, and her black guts kind of hanging out one side in between.

Every ounce of Emily's energy returned, as if she hadn't run for days. Hatred was rocket fuel. She forgot she was tired, and that she already exhausted all the morning's energy, and she bolted through the intersection and flew at the woman like a jet propelled by unfathomable rage.

They ended up in a heap with Emily straddled across the top of the other woman. The woman tried to reach up and grab hold, her pretty, black-veined face wriggling with surprise and distain, but Emily was too full of monster inside herself to let the woman get away. It was beyond control, beyond reason. Emily pulled back a fist and slammed it into the woman's grey cheek. Between her fist and the pavement, she felt the bones break, but, she hit her again and again, until all Emily could see was a mass of red and black. No more blood shot green eyes, and the woman's silky black ponytail was gore glued to the street. Even then, Emily swelled again with anger and found other parts of the woman to destroy that weren't as gruesome as her obliterated face.

Somewhere it drifted back, between ragged breaths and violence like fire.

Emily had known her.

She'd known her without knowing. She'd only seen her once, but that had been with Todd, wrapped up in his arms with her big, oozy boobs pressed against his chest, lips swallowing his face.

The memory, and she was sure it was a memory, did nothing to lessen her rage. She had limitless energy for annihilation, the excitement of bones breaking, and grey brain squishing and splatting on the sidewalk. It wasn't until Emily felt her knuckles hit the concrete that she felt the pain. It was inside and out, radiating from her hands to her heart and back again. Breathe.

Red snarled and thundered, and she almost didn't care. She wanted to keep punching until the pain that had come and flooded every corner of her had also gone away, except Red sounded so violent and afraid that she looked up from her shredded knuckles and the human sidewalk stain.

There were five of them. It was the worst possible time to remember she was exhausted, and her body was shaking with rage still yes, but now pain and fear, and tiredness multiplied exponentially by destruction.

One of them had wandered so close, he was already lunging down, reaching. She heard Red's bark rip the air as she rolled, only narrowly avoiding black fingers, and a yellow wrecking ball with teeth.

The space she had occupied was filled with snarling dog, and the area around them was shrinking by the second. Even if she could have gotten up fast enough to run, there was no direction where she wouldn't have to fight. She reached for the gun on her belt and hopped to her feet just as another one of them reached for her. Her fingers were swollen from driving them into bone and pavement. Gripping the gun to aim was difficult. Instead of trying to put some space between, she went straight into the snarling woman's arms and slammed the butt of the gun into her temple. Emily didn't have the strength to break through another skull, but still the woman dropped momentarily.

They had an opening but not for long. She grabbed Red by the back of the collar and jerked hard in the direction she wanted him to go. He got the message and detached his teeth from the man's face, which was mauled beyond looking face-like. Together, She and Red bolted through the overgrown yards, but they hadn't gone far when she realized that this way was blocked with a line of people, and the second they were seen, a small mob was reaching, yelping, coming too fast.

Her moment of hesitation was a moment too long. Before she could move again she felt a cold grip on her shoulder and nails digging in through her shirt. She felt the forward momentum, and she knew that she would fall, that the thing would be on her back and biting.

She should have been afraid. She should have felt the fear of dying, but all she felt was encroaching cold, filling in the spaces where her anger had been. All she could see was that woman's face pressed against Todd, and them both, so happy. Maybe it was better not to feel that pain. Maybe if she were like the others, with those empty blood shot eyes, she could live at last, not be alone, and put those memories to rest.

She looked at Red, circling, just waiting for a clean bite that would matter. She didn't want to leave him. Todd would never keep him, and he'd be alone again. There was no place where the loneliness did not penetrate.

There was a boom. For a second, she thought it had come from inside her. It felt like it had, and she felt the hand on her shoulder go lax and slip away. Just as Emily thought she would fall, as she was sure she would die, she only stumbled forward and found her feet again. Her feet wanted to live. The rest of her followed in waves.

Someone had shot the man who'd had hold of her. There was a hole in the side of his head. He was tall but shriveled on the ground with black and grey leaking from his hair and busted bone. There was no time to seek out her savior. Red had already charged a small woman with brown hair and she saw the streak of them hurtling for the ground.

She forced her swollen fingers into position on the gun and pointed it at their last pursuer who was in the rear because he was round and hobbling. She pulled the trigger, but it didn't feel right. Nothing happened.

"Son of a bitch." She flipped the safety. Red for dead, it fucking rhymed! This time the gun fired, and the man rolled backward like a squishy boulder. There was another boom from the rooftops. The line of people blocking the road ahead began to fall one by one. She walked toward the shrinking mob and aimed slow. Red circled her, doggie mohawk between his shoulders at attention and his mouth leaving drops of gore in a halo at her feet.

Her heart began to slow with the realization that she was almost free, and by the time the last one fell, she followed it to the ground. Without fear, she had nothing to keep the exhaustion at bay, and the muscles in her legs quivered against the street. She rolled her head to look at the line of bodies on the ground and then back the other way, to the woman she'd destroyed. But she couldn't dwell on Todd's dead girlfriend. She felt a burst of rage again but didn't have the time or energy to let it burn. A few houses away, a man climbed down from a garage roof with a rifle slung across his back and he walked awkwardly, she guessed from the swollen ankle in an ace bandage hidden by his boots. "Hello, Adam."

Jessica. It was all still water still leaking through the dam. The girl she'd turned to pavement art, her name was Jessica, and Todd was an asshole.

There was little differentiation between those pieces of information. There was a black hole in her brain, one that sucked away her memories, it was closing in on itself, and soon it would be like she'd never forgotten at all.

Adam scratched Red and looked down at her balancing on his better foot. "Alive?"

"Yeah." She closed her eyes and opened them again, just in case, but he was still there. "You got a new gun." She struggled to catch her breath, but she stretched out a hand for him to help her up.

19

Adam took her hand and pulled her to her feet. They couldn't stay in the road in case there were more of the hungry. . . she couldn't bring herself to call them people. They weren't people anymore.

They climbed up onto a rooftop because it seemed the safest place, but they had trouble getting Red up there. He was heavy and squirmy, and liked heights about as much as could be expected of someone who'd spent life with mostly four feet on the ground. It took a few minutes, but once he'd found his footing on the shallow slope, he was as happy as ever. She was never going to be rid of that stain on his face. It grew a little redder every day.

Adam was more prepared for an outing than she had thought to be, and he had a backpack with water and food enough for the three of them. He seemed hesitant to say anything. She couldn't blame him. He probably thought she was crazy and may have just seen her crush some woman's face into the street.

In the quiet, she had time to look at him without distraction for the first time, and she realized that he was probably at least ten years younger than she was because, now that he was alone with her again, he seemed boyish and uncertain. She swallowed a piece of the granola bar he'd given her. "How did you find me?"

He went slightly red in the cheeks. "Not hard to find what you're following. Don't be angry. I've been keeping an eye out since that day at the plant."

She frowned. "Seriously?"

"It was Barbara's idea." He was quick to look away. "It's not like I just wanted to stalk you or anything, but Barbara said you might be sick, like head sick, and you might not be able to, you know, think rationally."

"I see." She took another bite and chewed thoughtfully. "I can't complain because you both probably just saved my life. There was a second there when I didn't want to get up again, so thanks."

"You saved me before. You don't have to thank me for anything. I was only able to be here today because of you."

"Did Barbara say what she thought was wrong with me?"

"She said it was something that couldn't be cured with penicillin. She thought you needed time, to process or remember. She didn't want me to get too close. She said you wouldn't get better if we pushed."

"She's smart." She tried to wipe her hands on her pants. It didn't clean them very much at all and the action was excruciating for her knuckles. "I feel better." She sighed. "And worse. Much worse than before."

"Do you want to talk about it?" He seemed immediately uncomfortable. "I mean, you don't have to. I don't want to pressure you, I just thought, never mind. I should shut up and eat my food."

Emily laughed a little. "You forgot how to talk to strange women, didn't you?"

Adam shook his head. "I never knew. If it didn't need motor oil and an engine, I was never much good at talking."

"I think I used to be good at it. I know I had a friend once. I think I had more than one." Emily crumpled up the wrapper of the granola bar and tucked it in her pocket. "It's hard to tell."

"You'll find yourself again."

"I'm not sure I want to," she said. "Now I'm the kind of person who kills people with my bare hands in the street."

Adam frowned, but tried not to, making his lips into a pancake instead. "You didn't kill her. Not exactly."

"Please, don't. . ."

"She was already dead, Emily."

Emily burst into tears so violently she nearly slipped off the roof. "They are. Everyone.

God." The words sputtered out of her between sobs. "Everyone is dead."

"Not everyone. Not you and me."

"But I feel dead. I can't remember so many things still, and every time I remember there's only misery. My best friend is gone." She struggled for a breath. "My parents. I don't even remember my parents. Not really. It's like I just deleted them from my head because I couldn't stand it. I couldn't stand the good memories, and now all I have are bad ones."

Adam dug around in his bag for a small package of tissues. "I get allergies." He extended them awkwardly toward her.

She took the tissues, and he let her cry. By the time the flood had begun to subside, he was staring off in the direction of the sun.

"I'm sorry." She sniffled. "I shouldn't be unloading on you. This isn't your problem."

"We all went through it. No one alive now lives without a few holes in their heart. I know what you're thinking. How could I forget? How can I just go on like nothing happened, but at some point, we all had to give up or go on. People change when the world changes.

"But it hasn't. It was so easy to let go because nothing changed. I never knew my neighbors. We smiled and waved, but once the front door closes it's like the lights shut out on the rest of the planet. This has always been a world of mostly silent, hungry strangers. They all had lives in their own little worlds locked behind the front door. The only difference now is that they reach out more."

Adam nodded. "I can probably count on two hands the number of people who really knew me. Even less if I only count the ones who really cared. When it happened, me and my girlfriend, Bethy, were camping. She was super smart, much too smart for me. She was getting a degree in Biology and Chemistry, and she wanted to work with endangered animals, so we were always out in the sticks somewhere looking for some stupid turtle or owl that she wanted to see.

"We'd heard the first reports for a week, some weird thing in Brazil they were calling Dunn-Hitchens disease. So stupid. It sounds like the sort of obscure thing people hold fundraisers for, you know, like a telethon for DHD awareness or something.

"Bethy couldn't stop reading about it. She said it was spreading, and people should start taking precautions, but the only thing they did was issue a travel warning for people who might want to visit a DHD affected area.

"We had been gone about a week, hiking, feeling like we were the only people on earth. Then my mother called. Don't come home, she said, and I said why not, and she said because of that disease. It was like it exploded. One minute it was some isolated thing and the next minute-mom said there were riots. She said the military was keeping people off the streets, evacuating.

"Then she told me my dad had got it, that he was showing all the signs, tiredness, inattentiveness, and his skin was so pale it looked grey. I wasn't supposed to come home. They said I'd catch it, or it would catch me."

Emily was clenching her eyes closed so tightly it hurt. As he spoke, her brain was gluing fragments of glass together as thin as needles, it was his story but. . .

Adam saw the expression on her face. "Should I shut up?"

Emily wanted to tell him yes. She didn't want to hear, or remember, or think. Tears slid out of her eyes without blinking and she ran her fingers through Red's fur. "I told Todd I needed the truth. Please keep telling me the truth. Don't stop. Even if I cry, or scream, or throw myself off this roof, tell me truth."

Adam nodded, and hugged himself with both arms. "At first, we listened. Mom said Dad wasn't so bad, and for four days, she called me, and said he was feeling better all the time."

Emily felt a swell of anger. "She lied."

"Because she loved me." Adam looked up at the sky and then down at the laces on his boots.

"It doesn't matter. Lies hurt the most from people you love."

Adam dipped his chin and drew his knees closer to his chest. His long legs made him look like a shriveled scarecrow. "On the fifth day, she didn't call. I knew she was gone. I can't tell you how I knew, but I did, and I lied to myself. I told myself she'd probably forgotten because dad was so much better, she didn't think of it. And we packed up and went home."

"Did your girlfriend hear from her parents?"

"Bethy grew up in foster care. She was basically alone, and she lied to me too. She told me not to worry, even though she had to know better. She was too smart not to know.

"We headed home, and when we got closer to town we saw the planes and the smoke. The jets were burning out the dead in the center of town, and there was chaos on the roads. We had to walk the last two miles, and we were lucky not to get caught. But we didn't see a single one of them the whole way, until I got home.

"Mom was in her nightgown. Dad had taken off more than a chunk of her, but she was still walking. Mom went for Bethy, and Bethy jumped out of the way. I went to the coat closet for my Dad's old shotgun, but I couldn't do it. She was my mom, even if she was trying to eat us.

"I think that was the stupidest thought I had my whole life. While I was sitting there, pointing a shotgun at my mom's face, hoping she didn't take a bite out of me, and thinking about how much I loved her, my Dad had come down the stairs for Bethy. She screamed, but not for long. Dad went right for her throat.

"Two minutes, and all the people I could name that really loved me were gone. I shot my mother, I shot my father, and then, I shot Bethy, because she was bleeding out and there was nothing I could do, and I didn't want to see her get up again. I had nowhere to go. I didn't know what I was supposed to do."

"And the world was full of strangers." Emily put a hand on his knee and offered him his tissues back.

Adam took them and tucked them back in his bag. He stared straight ahead and said nothing, and she thought if he stayed in that position forever he'd scare away all the birds. He might as well have been a rag doll made of cloth and paper.

"The woman, I mean the thing, what I did back there, she wasn't a stranger."

"You knew her?"

"Before it happened, my husband, Todd, was screwing her. I saw her, I remembered, I couldn't stop myself."

There was an unmistakable hint of confusion in his voice. "And you two are still married?"

"Well that's the thing, isn't it? I shouldn't

be. I wouldn't have forgiven him. I barely trusted him before. I would have gotten divorced. There wouldn't have even been a conversation. I know this about myself, it's one of the few things in me that are immovable."

"If it makes you feel any better, I don't think divorce is a thing anymore."

She gave him half a smile. "I can barely forgive him for leaving a pair of boxers on the floor. There's no way I knew about this and everything was okay. I think I asked him for a divorce before. I must have. Todd always wears his wedding band. But I don't have a ring. I don't remember what happened to it exactly. I feel like I took it off, but he's still around, and I can't remember why."

"Because you love him?"

"I can't be in love with someone who isn't in love with me."

"You could leave. The plant has room. You don't have to be the only people in the world anymore."

There were so many things she wanted to do, go with Adam to the plant and just disappear, go home and empty a magazine into Todd's lying mouth, but none of those things would give her what she needed. "I can't make decisions when I can't think. I need to remember. I need my truth."

"You will remember everything eventually."

"Will you keep following me?"

He drew his eyebrows up in surprise. "You want me to follow you?"

"I don't want to forget again. If it seems like I am the way I was before, I want you to take me and make me listen. Don't lie to me. Don't let me lie to me, and if you have time, maybe also keep shooting anything that gets too close."

"I will have one kidnapping ready and waiting. Please don't shoot me."

Emily laughed. "I'll try not to forget."

"You want me to walk you home?"

"No. You need to take it easy on that foot. I won't go jogging anymore."

"Yeah, that hurt."

"Just help me get Red down and let me think I'm alone."

"No. You told me not to lie to you."

"Then take a day off and stalk me again tomorrow."

They climbed down, much to Red's irritation, and walked together as long as their paths were the same. They walked in silence because Emily was walking through a world she'd never seen before.

She lost count of broken windows she'd never noticed, cars empty, run off the road, and abandoned with their doors open. Everything had begun to rust and warp, and it was impossible not to feel the emptiness or see the strangers everywhere. The dead haunted the windows, pacing back and forth. The dead lurked and sulked and shambled. They spoke, but not like before.

Because now she could hear sorrow instead of words, and pity, and suffering in the hollow moans that followed her home. At the end of her street, her own private avenue of strangers, she didn't feel like she was coming home.

All these people that she'd never known, that she'd wondered about in passing, whispered about in gossip, all the children limping in the tall grass, she'd never seen them as human, not even when they were. She never said hello, except to wave and leave them in their little worlds of ones and twos, and hopes and sadness, and love and loneliness.

No more.

She decided and acted in the same moment. Emily kicked through the wooden fence to the back yard of the first house on the street. There was a little girl, a dead little girl that looked like she'd been buried once but clawed back out again. Emily didn't think. She fired. Mercy.

In the house, she found the girl's father, but no mother. There were only pictures of him and the little girl, some sheet music strewn across the bench of a piano. "Hello," she said, and gave him peace.

It was her last bullet, but no matter. She

found a heavy hammer in the garage and cleaver in the kitchen drawer. She took them both.

The next house was empty, but the house after that had two teenage boys inside. There were pictures of them in football uniforms all over the place, but no sign of their parents. She dug the cleaver in to both of them in turn and they landed together in a pile on living room carpet.

An hour later, she had finally met all her neighbors. And they had all been beautiful people in their own private ways. There was only one house left to clear.

She went through her front door and in to the back yard for the stepladder because she knew Mr. Johnson would still be outside.

Quietly, she climbed up the ladder to peer over the fence. Mr. Johnson had his back turned to her, and he looked almost human. She wished she could leave him, she wished she could stand on the fence and talk to him again no matter how naked he was. "Mr. Johnson." He turned, his head first, and then his body, because he couldn't manage both at the same time.

"I don't know if I would've been okay without you. You were a good friend, for a dead guy." He reached the fence, pressing himself into it, craning up to look at her, his arms awkwardly flailing. "But I'm okay now. And you are too."

He said nothing in return. She'd never heard him speak, not really. Even when he was alive, and they were neighbors, they'd never so much as said good morning. She brought the cleaver down on the back of his head, pinning him between the blade and the cinder block fence. The wound wasn't very deep, and it took a little time for him to stop flailing and go lax. He fell on his back in the overgrown grass, his bloodshot eyes staring straight up at the sun, and his nasty bathrobe splayed out beneath him like a picnic blanket. The others on the street she'd left where they'd fallen, but Mr. Johnson had been her friend, his corpse at least. Him, she would find the strength to bury.

20

She waited for Todd sitting on the second stair. Now that she knew, she couldn't help but wonder what he did at work all day. There was nothing interesting at the hardware store to keep him occupied for eight hours a day without any actual work to do. She was sure some of it was just to keep up the ruse of his imaginary world, but part of her just wondered if he wanted to escape her. Still another part suspected he might be just as crazy as she was, and as always, a large, and very familiar part wanted to bash him in the head.

And his employees, all dead and zip tied around the store. She felt nauseous thinking about it. Why not just kill them?

He got home at his usual time, but of course there was practically nothing to throw off his routine. She watched the doorknob turn and heard the jangle of his keys. It was amazing how swiftly the familiar had changed. He pushed open the door to find her sitting there. His eyes were bright and unsuspicious. Proof, she thought, that he didn't know her at all. "Hey," he said with a thin smile.

The sight of his smile renewed her nausea.

"How long have you known?"

"Known what, babe?"

Not this time. She couldn't bear his nonchalance, his easy unconcern. "How long have you known that everything, everyone, was gone?"

Todd frowned and closed the door behind him. "I don't think you really want to talk about this."

"So- always. You knew." She reached out to grip a post of the stair railing. "I hoped it wasn't true. I wanted so much to hope, but there's almost no such thing now, is there?"

"Don't be ridiculous."

She snorted. "Don't lie to me, and don't try to make me think I'm crazy, because I might have been before, but I'm sure as hell not now."

Todd's voice was completely cold. "Of course, I've known."

"I wanted to think it wasn't only me, that maybe you'd forgotten too, at least at first."

Todd's face was haughty and impatient. "There are a lot of things you don't want to be true. And even more we want that can't ever be."

Emily only nodded and stared at the wall above Todd's head. She tried to find her own coldness, her own piece of casual cruelty. "I saw Jessica today. Did you know she's dead?"

"I don't know what you're talking about."

"Another lie." She felt her face twist into both smile and sneer. He was getting frustrated, and she thought it was the best thing he could feel next to shame. "Yes, you knew her, Todd. You knew her in that extra special cheating bastard husband sort of way. Well, I saw her, and I put her down." She held both of her fists out for him to see the blood and bruising. "I broke her face with my hands because I saw her and remembered her with you."

"Jesus. Em. This? We can't go through this again. We've already been through. For fuck's sake if there was one thing to remember, it's this. You saw me. I admitted I cheated, and you were pissed for a while, justifiably livid, but not forever. You forgave me. You said you still loved me."

"How am I supposed to believe you? Everything you tell me is a lie. I remember telling you we were getting divorced. I remember filling out the paperwork and handing it you. I remember taking off my ring."

"You did, you did all those things, Em but we tore the paperwork up. You forgave me, and we tore it up together."

"I couldn't have forgiven you."

"But you did. I thought you wouldn't either, but you did."

Emily grabbed the railing post again and dug her nails into the wood. "Why do you keep lying to me?"

"I'm not. This time. This time it's the truth." From his place at the top of the stairs, Red growled. She hadn't washed the blood off either of them, and she wondered if Todd knew how close he was to having his throat ripped out like a squeaky little chew toy.

She narrowed her eyes. "Even if I could believe you this time, it wouldn't make up for everything."

"You should be thanking me for lying to you. All I did was protect you. I protected you from yourself, and I protected you from the truth because the truth was fucking ugly. What was I supposed to say? Your parents are dead. My brother, my mom and dad, our-" He stopped and took a slow, deep breath.

"Yes, you were supposed to tell me." She spat out the words. "What right did you have to keep it from me, to decide what I should get to feel." She was so angry she could feel her lips trembling.

"You'd blocked it out, Em, not me. So, I let you, and I lied. Anyone who loved someone as much as I love you would have done the same. I had to go through it. I had to see it all, to feel it. I didn't get to forget. I had to watch the world burn down around me, and I remember all of it. All I wanted was to keep you from that pain."

"It might have hurt. It might have killed me, but it was my pain to feel, and you kept it from me. You kept me locked up in this prison of wallpaper and lies."

"You don't understand. You don't remember. But I know I did the right thing. If I had to, I'd make the same choice again."

It was difficult to ignore his desperation, the strange fragments of honesty and conviction slipping through him into the air, but pain, the pain he denied her, was a cure for many things. "I know you would. That's why I have to leave. I'm going to be with the others. I don't care what you do. Live here. Die here. Lie to yourself and think that none of this was your fault, but I am leaving."

"Others?" The sudden fear that caused Todd's voice to crack made her sit back from him.

She drew her eyebrows together, trying to figure out if he was in the process of spinning something new into his lies. "Yes, Todd. There are others. There's a group. The man I saved took me to them and showed me I wasn't alone with you. Did you think you were the last person on Earth, or hope you were?"

"Em, I'd rather be the last person on Earth than let you do this." Todd backed toward the door, blocking it with his body. She watched a bead of sweat run down his face. The fear, the concern, it looked so genuine, but even that, she could not trust.

"It's not your decision."

He pressed his body against the door as hard as he could.

"I will go through you if I have to."

196

"Em." He sighed. "If you want to leave, I can't stop you, but first, just listen. I know it's coming back to you, but you don't remember everything. I can tell you. I will tell you anything you want to know."

She stood up. "I'd rather go and live in the dump than let you fill it in for me. I can't trust a word you say."

"We've already tried living with other people. Please, Em. You can't trust them. It's going to end in misery."

"Then what difference does it make?" She huffed. "The same thing will happen if I stay." She reached for the door, and like a child, he pressed himself into the corner. Red trotted past him cowering there and followed Emily to the SUV.

21

She had meant to be so strong, to drive straight to the plant like she knew it was her destiny, but at the first intersection that would have started her on that path, she couldn't force herself to make the turn. She sat at the corner so long the dead came. She let them smack at the windows and stared at their black-veined, snapping faces while she tried to think.

Emily wished she could delete Todd from her brain, and wondered, with all the other things she'd managed to forget, why he'd be the one thing that stayed. She wanted to write it off as something easy. She remembered because she'd seen him every day. She remembered because he caused her as much pain as anyone could feel, surely, but still not enough to drive him from her brain. Red whined in the seat beside her, mohawk in full bloom.

Aside from the plant, there was nowhere else to go, and she couldn't get the look on Todd's face out of her mind when she'd told him there were others.

There were a lot of things that Todd could fake, but fear seemed unlikely. She wondered why it was fear and not surprise. He spent so much time out of the house, it was possible he knew that there were other people alive. The idea only made her trust him less and hate him more.

But she still couldn't make herself drive toward the plant. Red did an impatient little dance in the seat as another of the dead approached the passenger side.

She stroked his shoulders and told him it would be okay, then drove for the one other place she remembered ever feeling completely safe.

Danny's house was as empty as she'd last left it. She went through the side gate and let herself in the back after stopping for a minute to look down at Danny's grave.

The house wasn't exactly a fortress, especially now that Emily had broken out the kitchen window, but it was good enough for an hour or two. She wandered through the empty rooms, running her fingertips over furniture and picture frames, like something in the house might contain some magic she could take into herself.

Every now and then, she found a fracture of a memory, but nothing that could make her feel any more complete. She found a framed picture of Danny and herself, which she removed. Danny no longer needed the memory, and Emily didn't think Danny would mind.

She sat down on Danny's sofa, an over-stuffed tan affair, and pulled her knees into her chest so she could feel as small as possible. Red jumped up in the seat beside her and laid as close as he could. He looked up at her with raised, sympathetic eyebrows, and she put one hand on his head to try and reassure him she was okay. Red was much too smart to believe that. "Stop looking at me that way. I'm allowed to not be okay."

'Of course, you are. I don't blame you at all.'

She looked down at the dog, knowing full well that he hadn't said or heard anything. And really, she hadn't heard it either; it was an echo of a memory.

This is where she'd come when she'd left Todd the first time. Of course, it was. She'd had no real place to go before any more than she had now, and the only person she would have trusted with that much pain was now buried in the back yard. But the memory, that much at least, was alive inside the house. Emily closed her eyes and tried hard to imagine Danny as she remembered her, sitting in the armchair next to the sofa holding a cup of coffee. 'Do you love him?'

"I don't know." Emily said to the air. "I can't love someone who doesn't love me."

'If you thought he didn't love you, you wouldn't be asking me.'

"How could he love me if he would do this to me?"

Danny had smiled wickedly over her coffee cup. 'He's never been particularly smart.'

They'd laughed, even while Emily was crying. "I don't know what to do."

'Because there's more to the two of you than just this thing.'

"I don't know if I can forgive him."

Danny had given her another mischievous grin. 'Well I won't, but I'm allowed to hate every ounce of his ass for the rest of his life.' A moment of silence had passed between them. 'You don't have to decide now. You don't have to think about it all as one big thing. That's too much. Right now, you only need to decide if you want to try to forgive him. Maybe you won't. Maybe you'll go home and months from now you'll bop him over the head with something and just leave. But that comes later, after you decide if you want to try.'

"I don't want to try. I could never trust him again. I never will, but I'll try. . ." Emily had run out of memory, but it was enough at least to believe Todd might have told her the truth about that one thing. She had gone back to him. If she'd tried to forgive him, maybe try had led to succeed.

And if she'd done it once, then maybe she could do it again. Even if all the pain was new all over, and it felt like the flood of anger would never recede. If she was only willing to try, then maybe.

She wiped one eye and stood up from the sofa. "Love you, Danny." Emily spoke to the empty house and hoped the love would somehow reach the memory. Red jumped down, always ready to follow where she might lead. "Come on, baby. Let's go home and maybe kill Todd, or let him live, or love him. We'll just have to see."

It wasn't until she left the house that she realized how long she'd been inside. The sun was already setting, and it was dangerous to run around much without being able to see. They made it back to the SUV and drove toward home, but the road had changed in the hours she'd spent inside Danny's. There was a large group of dead children that had wandered into the street by the elementary school, and though she knew she'd be doing them a favor, she couldn't bring herself to run them down.

Instead, she turned on to what she quickly realized was a familiar street, but it wasn't the scenery that brought her to recognition, it was a feeling of fear so fervent she had to pull over and open the car door long enough to vomit into the street.

Red looked disgusted.

"You eat dead people. Don't judge me." She said wiping her mouth with the back of one hand and pulling the door closed with the other.

She sat back in the seat and tried to let the feeling pass, but it was slow to recede. She didn't know the name of the streets that made up the intersection where she'd stopped, and she couldn't tell because a large tan military vehicle had turned over and taken out the street sign.

There was something about the overturned truck. She'd driven by it before, but it had never seemed any more important than all the other cars left to rust in the streets. But the world had changed, and now the truck was almost hypnotic. She opened her car door again and climbed out, careful to avoid the pool of vomit beside the car. Red followed her out, not content to let her go on her own and not at all happy to be out in the dark.

She heard an awkward squawk and saw a few large vultures pecking at a body that had been mostly eaten from the arms down, and the head, still alive and chomping, desperately trying to eat the things that were eating it.

"Weird time to be a vulture." She said to one of the birds. Then, she circled the truck and put a hand on a thick tire to thumb at the tread. Adam said there had been an evacuation, or at least they tried to evacuate. She couldn't remember which. There was a cover over the truck bed made of thick cloth, but it was shredded and bloody in several places. The driver's side door was slightly open, and there was no one in the cab. Maybe the drivers got away.

No. That didn't feel right.

The drivers were dead. Their bodies were gone. There was a bloody M4 laying near an overgrown shrub. She picked it up and checked the magazine, still loaded, but almost empty. Then she walked to the back again, and despite every urge to stop immediately and go straight back to the safety of the SUV, she lifted the shredded cover over the truck bed with the barrel of the rifle.

The smell was so overwhelming even Red backed away. Inside, the bodies had bloated and split open before the sun had baked the whole mess into a sort of dry human tortilla around the bones. It was difficult to tell one hard roasted body from another but at least two of them were soldiers; she could tell by the uniforms, but the rest. . .

Emily gagged and dropped the canvas, but it was too late. The sight had already branded her eyes. She knew them. Not exactly. She knew their faces, even almost dry to the skull some of them were familiar. Some of them she'd waved to every now and then, and others, she'd seen in photographs on the walls of the houses on her street as she'd gone through and done the messy work of mercy. All those empty houses were empty because their owners were packed together in the back of the truck meant to save them.

And she'd hid behind them when the dead came. The convoy had gone on when the one vehicle had crashed, and the soldiers up front had climbed out and tried to fight the dead away.

It was the sound. The streets were crowded

with those monsters and the guns only drew more of the dead's attention, so they came in a slow swarm and surrounded the truck. The soldiers had stopped firing, and there was nothing left to eat but their fragile human cargo.

She'd cowered in the back, too terrified even to scream, and stuck on the idea that she shouldn't have left home no matter how much she'd been urged and ordered to leave.

She knew she was going to die, and she'd started to say goodbye in her mind to all the things that had made her human, and she'd clutched her things to her chest, as if a blanket, a bag, and a few pairs of jeans would somehow shorten the grisly ending that awaited her when the dead chewed through the others.

But just as she thought she'd do nothing but surrender, she fought. One of the others pressed against the back of the truck with her handed her a piece of pipe, and they stayed alive a few more seconds with each swing at the skulls of the dead. There was the sound of gunfire again, and she thought, thank God the soldiers have come back for us, but when the dead had fallen there were no more soldiers. There was Todd, wearing his hardware store polo and a pair of blood-spattered jeans.

"How did you find me?"

"Luck."

"Let's stay lucky."

He'd saved her, and two others who had survived the crash and the onslaught of the dead. The others, he helped into the truck bed, but her, he lifted into the cab and closed the door, and kept her safe.

22

When Emily got home, Todd was sitting on the sofa in the family room staring at a blank TV. He looked sunken and pale, and he said nothing when she sat down and nothing when Red growled at him before jumping between him and Emily.

Emily stroked Red's Mohawk and tried to tell them both that things might be okay. Finally, Todd looked at Red and then slowly up at Emily. "Do you hate me?" He blinked and looked more tired than she had ever seen.

"No."

"But you don't love me."

"I did. Now, I don't know. It's too soon to think. I know that we've been through it. I believe that we didn't go through with the divorce, and I came home, and we tried to work on things. But I don't remember how I forgave you. All I remember is the hurt. It's old to you, but it's new again to me."

He seemed to try and nod but could not escape gravity to lift his chin again. "You forgave me once. You won't do it again."

"Last time, I thought maybe things would

change, but they didn't. You lied and kept lying."

"I just wanted to protect you, Em."

Already she regretted coming home. "Still lies. You don't lie to me to keep me safe, Todd. You lie to me because you think I'm weak. How can I believe you love me if your opinion of me is that I'm going to crumble at the slightest thing?"

Todd spoke, but there was no fight in him. They were just words, in empty space, in their empty house. "You are weak. It's not an opinion, it's a fact. If you weren't weak, you wouldn't have listened to me. You wanted to forget. You wanted to believe me."

The wind had picked up outside and rattled the glass of the back door and shook the garden leaves. Red stirred unhappily in his seat. "I didn't forget on purpose, Todd. What other option did I have if the one person who could have set me straight would only lie to me?"

"You're less mad about me lying than you are about my doing it without your permission. But you were fucked up, Em. You weren't thinking. And I was fucked up. What else was I supposed to do?"

"Try and heal me, not keep me sick."

"I did try." He said sadly, his arms dead weight at his side. "For a while. When we first came home, it was like you were haunting the house. You drifted from room to room, looking at the pictures on the walls, looking right through me. You said the pictures hurt you, so I took them away. I told you that your parents were dead, and you laughed at me. You told me I wasn't funny. Then it was like you didn't even have parents. You asked me once if I knew what happened to Danny. I didn't know, and then it was like she was gone too. Everything that made you happy, everyone who meant anything, you just wiped them away.

"There were moments, Em, when I'd make you see. I think it was only those times you ever really hated me, because I made you think about it. You would cry and scream, and the dead would come and rap at the windows. I'd have to lead them away. You made me choose for you because you couldn't do it yourself. I chose to keep you safe. All I wanted was for us to be safe and happy."

"It was more than that, Todd. Don't try and make me feel sorry for you. You didn't do it only for me. You don't have a bone of real selflessness in you. You had to get something out of keeping me here and keeping me stupid."

"I got you, Em."

"Since when I was enough for you?"

"Since everything changed."

"You mean because the world changed?"

"No, people. People changed."

"You have one chance left to tell me the truth, Todd. I'm here. I'm listening."

Todd nodded like the truth might actually

kill him and every word was suicide. "There were four sites at first. The stadium at the high school only lasted a few days. They weren't careful. Someone infected got in, turned in the night and there was nothing to do but drop a bomb on the place. So that's what they did.

"The others took longer. A rec center on the edge of town lasted almost three weeks before a fence came down and they were gone. Soon there was only the prison and the base. The prison lasted almost six weeks before their supplies ran out. Some people talked about helping them, but food was so difficult to replace.

"We lost contact with the prison, and when they finally sent someone for a fly over, all they saw were bodies and the dead wandering through the guard gate.

"The base was overcrowded. A place meant for five hundred men and suddenly there were five thousand. We slept on the ground in the open. There were no showers, we made ditches for toilets. It made a lot of people sick.

A few of the old ones and some of the kids died. The soldiers threw them over the fences to let the dead dispose of them.

The soldiers had lost contact with everyone. They argued among themselves about what to do. Words became demands, demands became fights, fights became murder, and the guy that took charge of it all, he just decided.

"No one on the base who couldn't work or fight. Those that were too old or too sick were sent away. A few soldiers went at a time, and only the soldiers came back."

Emily could see every word he spoke like one of his dumb movies flickering through her mind. "They didn't just kill them." She shuddered. "They used them as bait to lure away the dead."

Todd nodded. "And then they went through the rest of us one by one, to make sure we had a reason to stay."

"You told them you knew about solar, and you could get the power on. And when they got to me, I didn't have anything to say. He looked at me like I was some little thing he could crush with his boot heal. I told him I could grow things."

Todd looked away at the wind whipping through her garden. "He told you a lot of people could grow things."

"And then I told him I could handle a rifle. He laughed at me. He handed me his rifle like it was some kind of joke."

She'd had to prove it. Emily felt like water all over. The rifle seemed unnaturally heavy, and her hands were trembling so violently that she could barely steady the scope enough to look through it. That asshole laughed at her again.

Hatred made her steady. Venom made her stone. She took aim at one of the dead piled up on the fence about 100 yards away. She breathed like her father had taught her during hunting season when she was a little girl, and she prayed like her mother had taught her every Sunday. She squeezed the trigger and caught the dead man just above the ridge of one eyebrow through the hole in the chain link.

"Well holy shit." The soldier had said with a cold little smile "I love a good surprise." He pulled the rifle from Emily's quaking grasp and walked away.

Emily blinked at Todd, still sitting there like he was made of lead. "They took everyone else away. More bait. But they let us stay."

"I'm tired, Em. Can't we just. . .

"No."

Todd blinked. It seemed to take longer than usual to accomplish even that. "They put you in a guard tower. You were great. You helped keep them off the fences, and you were the best they had. That was a good thing. Other people, sometimes they complained. The ones that complained too much ended up outside the gate.

"People were on edge. People, afraid. Only certain people could carry guns because a lot of people shot themselves, so they didn't have to die and get up again.

"It had to end eventually; everyone knew. And I knew we'd be glad you had a rifle when the end finally came."

"I was in the tower." Emily blinked, the

memory appearing unbroken in her brain. "I got bored up there. I used to watch the dead through the fence when they were too far away. There was one guy who'd been eaten through at the middle before he'd risen and eaten someone else. He sat on the ground with his guts splayed out, watching the flesh he consumed come out the hole in his middle. Each time, he made a face like he'd just won the jackpot on a slot machine. He just kept eating the chunks again. He looked up, so I looked up, and I saw the plane."

It had been weeks since anything flew over. It was a little turbo prop, the kind used for airport hopping or private pilots with money to waste. It teetered in the air as though it slid along an invisible balance beam with its wings tipping precariously. Its nose began to dip, and it curved downward like it was made of paper instead of steel.

At some point, she realized it was coming down, but she'd already begun to move, instinct quicker than consciousness. The wail of the engines as the plane dove drowned out everything she in her head. She couldn't think, but she moved, and with all the speed that terror and adrenaline could manage.

She was out of the tower and running toward the solar array, toward Todd before the plane clipped the tower and spread splintered wood and flame as it broke into pieces and barreled into the fence at the front gate. Metal met metal and they twisted together with a grim screech. Chaos spread with the smoke, and people ran, some to try and put the fires out, some to bark orders or flee from them, and some ran for the gate where the tangled fence and fractured plane had punctured their fragile illusion of being safe.

The higher the flames rose, billowing black into the sky, the more effective the beacon became, and from every side, even the laziest dead sputtered toward the fences. By the time she reached the array, she could hear gunfire and knew that it meant the dead had discovered their vulnerability.

Todd wasn't at the array. No one was, except a few taking their chances with the barb wire to escape. She didn't pause even an instant. There was no force that could have stopped her feet. She arced back the other way, toward the bunk they shared at the barracks. The buildings were like an old-style hotel with doors that opened onto a shared walkway. She nearly mowed people down as a few who had been sleeping stumbled out into day.

Their room was empty. Here she was forced to double over and divert energy to her brain. People were generally flowing away from the gunfire, and though it seemed safer to ride a wake of bullets, she thought that Todd would not have gone that way. He'd be looking for her, so once again, she ran, back to where she'd first come down from the tower.

The area was hot and filled with a growing number of dead investigating the flames for barbecue, but she found him, alive and charging toward her. "I saw the plane, and then I found you."

"You wanted to head for the gate, but I remembered the other tower. I was so stupid. Even if we could have climbed to the top of it, we'd have to jump down again on the other side. We'd probably have ended up dead or broken and then dead. But it didn't matter. There were a lot of people as stupid as me. The tower was overrun, and it was too late to head for the front gate. It turned out it didn't matter anyway. They couldn't get through to the tower because too many people had thought the same thing. We went for the chain-link."

"I got up and over because I was small."

"Like a blond little monkey. But I wasn't small. I tried so hard." Todd choked.

"But you made it. You finally made it over. And we were okay."

"No." She wasn't sure if it was sweat or a tear that ran down his face. "You weren't okay. Everything had changed. I was looking at the same person. It was your face, but you weren't there anymore. I tried to get you running, but you just stood there. Then you turned to me and said-"

"I want to go home."

"So, I brought you home."

Emily took a few slow, deep breaths and tried to think, but it was difficult with the wind shaking the windows and doors. He was telling her the truth, but. . .

It didn't feel right. She was still a puzzle with a fuzzy picture and missing pieces. She was sure it was the truth, but not all of it.

And Todd knew it too, because he'd looked away. He couldn't lie to her. He didn't have the strength. If she had known what to ask him, she would have forced it out until she felt he'd sufficiently explained everything, but she didn't know where to begin or how to spot the discoloration on the history he painted.

He still stared out at her garden. Strange, she thought, because he'd never taken comfort in that place. She stared at him intently, letting the thunder of nature write the soundtrack to their silence. When he said nothing further, and the shadow from the clouds outside had covered his entire face, she finally decided to speak. "You aren't telling me everything."

"Emily, please."

He sounded so pathetic. Weak. His weakness was the fuse that lit her up again. "What is it with you? Is it impossible to tell me the truth? Have you lied so much you've forgotten how?"

Todd scowled. "I don't want to talk about it anymore than you want to hear about it."

"But I do want to hear it." She said quietly. "I want to hear everything."

Todd pressed his lips together, and with shaking fingers, wiped away sweat on his forehead.

Red growled fiercely at the movement of Todd's hand. She suspected he'd spent one too many storms outside and was now afraid of them. It made sense to Emily, with the dead, he could just rip their faces off, but wind and rain had no tender, meaty place to put his teeth.

Todd stared at Red morosely. "The dog is never going to like me, is he?"

"No. He's too much like me." She rubbed Red's ears. "Can't love someone who doesn't love him back."

"That and the blood in his teeth." Todd sulked, slumping further onto the sofa.

"I don't need to bite you. But that doesn't mean I don't need to leave."

He had no reaction except to chew his lip and look with exhaustion at their carpet. "I love you, Emily."

She knew she couldn't answer him, and she struggled with what she could say that wouldn't sound cruel or hurt him too much. If she loved him any more at all, it was buried somewhere like all her other memories, too deep to access, and too dark to see.

The storm saved her from having to speak. With a menacing crack, the wind ripped a branch off a tree in the front yard and whipped it into the window. They heard the glass shatter and wood splinter. As tired as he looked, Todd was instantly on his feet.

He dashed into the front room to examine the busted window. There wasn't much glass on the carpet. The branch had penetrated the window but not the boards behind it. Still, it was too uncomfortable a breach.

"I'll fix it." Todd was as eager to be busy as he was to be free from keeping their conversation going any longer.

"Should I help you?"

"No. I'll do it. It won't take ten minutes."

He hurried out the front door before she could say anything else. She heard him open the garage and close it again.

She spread out on the sofa. Her head felt heavy, like someone had poured molten lead inside her skull. Red insisted on laying down beside her, forcing her back into the couch cushions. He too seemed tired, but he showed no willingness to sleep. Instead, he watched the front door as if he were going to leap at Todd the minute he returned.

"You can't eat him baby." Red snapped his teeth with disappointment. "Not yet anyway."

Cheryl Loudermelt

23

By the time Todd came in from boarding up the outside of the window, she was nearly asleep. Todd stretched out on the other end of the sofa, and Red moved so that he was directly in between. She wanted to push Todd to tell her more, really, to tell her anything, but he was tired too, and there was no point in pressing onward that would warrant not getting a little bit of sleep.

Emily didn't dream at all, which was both a disappointment and a relief, but her respite was too brief to be grateful. Red's sharp, livid bark was all the alarm she'd ever need. She knew they were in trouble before she even opened her eyes. She woke up and moved in the same moment, but there was only so far to go.

There were six of them, spread between the sofa and the front door, which was wide open and shifting in the wind.

Todd was closer, and fortunately Red's warning had awoken him as well. Todd wasn't completely unarmed. He usually carried a knife on his belt, and he heaved the huge man who lurked down on him away after pressing the knife behind his ear and into his brain.

It happened so quickly. Emily had little time to react, and Red, even less. The man's body fell like a meteor over the dog, and Red squealed in pain. Emily bent to move the body away from him, but simply taking away the weight did not restore the Dog's fight. Red limped in agony, unable to support himself on his front paw.

"Run." Todd said calmly squaring off with a tall woman in green scrubs. "Run, Emily."

She threw herself in front of Red as another man with silver hair lumbered toward him. She grabbed a poker from the rack by the fireplace and swung. The blow connected but didn't penetrate. Still, it threw the silver haired man off balance. She reared back and swung again. This time she heard the skull crack and the man fell face first at her feet.

She made the decision in a heartbeat. Todd had drawn the attention of the remaining four of their uninvited guests, she had to help him, but with Red unable to move, it would only take a moment for one of them to demolish him. She dropped the poker and scooped up Red by the belly. He felt like he weighed as much as she did, but she managed to shift him back against her body and bolt toward the door, knocking one of the dead away with her shoulder as she passed. Todd tried to cut through the opening too, and he was partially successful before they cluttered up their path to the door, where yet another of the dead appeared looming in the entrance.

"Run." Todd's voice was calm as rain.

That coldness, that placidity that had always driven her mad for want of feeling, slowed the slamming of her heart and strengthened her grip on Red.

The stairs were the only option, and her only opportunity to possibly save them all. She heard Todd struggling at the foot of the stairs, but it was so difficult to distinguish his grunts from the others.

She leapt up, one foot landing squarely between the stair railing, and threw herself and the dog over the banister. Red whimpered and landed on top of her like a yellow cannon ball, but she lifted herself and him again and bolted up the stairs. She didn't think about it; she didn't hesitate. She flung open the door at the top of the stairs and set him down on the first patch of empty floor. She almost turned around again without really seeing, and maybe it would have been better not to see at all.

The walls were baby pink. There was a white bassinet with pink ribbons. The wood was old, and the paint was chipped in places, but it had been a gift from her mother. It was her mother's bassinet, and her own, and then. . .

Emily reached down and touched the scar on her abdomen as though her insides might rip through it to the floor. She reached around and closed the door.

She struggled with herself, that black place inside her still unwilling to reveal its secrets. But she shredded all that remained with sheer will.

Her baby's name was Chloe.

With a ghostlike hand, Emily reached out and pulled the blanket from the bassinet. She fell to the floor and pressed it to her nose with both hands. The smell was everything, every missing piece. She lost all track of time. She forgot Red. She forgot Todd. She crawled to the dresser drawers and opened each one, taking out the tiny clothes inside by the handful and pulling them to her face. She leaned her head against the open drawer of the dresser, both arms wrapped around the baby's clothes like if she tried hard enough, the body that had once filled them would be pressed to her chest again.

Chloe had cried so much, and Emily had spent every second trying to keep her quiet while they hid from the dead and waited for the evacuation to reach their street. Todd hadn't answered his phone, and she and Chloe were alone.

It didn't matter if he didn't answer; she knew where he would be. The world was falling apart, and he still couldn't let that other woman alone. She'd only tried to forgive him for Chloe, but he did nothing but leave them alone and afraid. She told herself, when Chloe was a little older and could understand, she would leave Todd forever. Someday.

She'd wrapped Chloe tightly in a blanket and packed her diaper bag. She went to the window, the impulse to look for Todd insurmountable. All she saw was the military trucks at the end of the street going door to door. They were leaving the infected, shooting the dead, and leaving them in the street.

She'd scribbled a note to Todd and left it on the TV. Looking at the soldiers in their uniforms, their sleeves dotted with blood and black, she'd doubted she would ever see Todd again.

She had tried for Chloe's sake, pressed into the back of the truck as far against the cab as she could squeeze. It seemed like the safest place, which was only about as safe as standing in the garden shed in the middle of a hurricane.

And she felt that way again, with her arms full of empty baby things. Downstairs, she heard a body crash into something, and wondered if it was Todd, or the dead, or if it mattered either way.

No. At least he'd tried. He did save them.

When the truck rolled over and she'd cowered against the cab with some of the others, while the rest were being ripped and devoured, and Chloe screamed in her arms. One of them handed her something hard and heavy, and she pressed Chloe to her chest with one arm and swung wildly to keep the dead at bay.

And Todd saved them and put them in the cab of his truck and took them to the base where he thought they'd be okay.

She wished he'd driven anywhere else, even if he'd driven them all straight into a lake that day. Because she'd fought to keep the baby quiet every time the soldiers came. Chloe was small and weak, and nonessential.

And forgotten, even by Emily.

24

The soldiers were difficult to keep at bay. She almost understood. Had she not been the object of their attention, she could have seen how desperate, angry men could end up that way. Todd couldn't leave her for a moment or they would come and harass her to set down the baby and come away with them. For fun, they called it. Hey honey, it's the end of the world...

Her mother had once told her that desperate men would say anything, but she tried not to think of her mother then. She didn't want to imagine black veins on the face of the woman she'd looked up at from the cradle.

Or her father, it was better to think of him in his overalls driving the big yellow tractor in the fields and waving as he passed her window.

One of the soldiers threatened to take the baby away. Todd had sheltered Chloe, but Emily had stood up and slung her fist right into the soldier's face.

He'd been so surprised and humiliated, all he'd done was scramble away to tell his friends a lie about the swelling already starting where her fist had landed.

"You shouldn't have." Todd said.

Emily reached down and took the baby away. "Next time, I'll kill him." Emily said in a sugary voice, speaking more to Chloe than Todd. "No one takes my Chloe away."

Later, it was the same soldier who came back to see what Todd and Emily had to offer to remain on the base. Todd glared at Emily when he saw that particular soldier walking their way. Emily thrust her jaw forward and clenched her teeth.

But she also prayed.

Todd held Chloe while she took the soldier's rifle. For a minute, she considered turning it on him and shooting that smug cruelty off his face. But instead, she aimed the rifle at the dead and prayed. The soldier took his rifle back and went away.

And there were days where she laid in the tower and watched that dead man eat the same meat he'd eaten for days and thought that it was the way the world worked, but she'd never noticed it. Every time people pulled ahead it would just fall through the bottom again; every day was a cycle of failure that seemed like success.

Their house, their cars, their tiny world wrapped in cinderblock, it was their carcass to eat and repeat. And it meant nothing, nothing to Todd, and almost nothing to Emily, except for Chloe. Emily would eat her own stomach if it meant that Chloe didn't have to live the same way.

That was the cruelty of it, really. Every parent thought that. Every parent ate their own misery to keep their children from pain, but the misery just came out the guts and the children grew up and took over the cycle of hoping and weeping. Even when the world fell apart, that much didn't change. It was the same place it had always been, a land of strangers in their private worlds eating their problems and pretending everything was okay.

Then she saw the plane.

This is the end of it. She watched it teeter in the sky. Finally. She'd have let it take her if it wasn't for Chloe.

Todd had Chloe.

She ran to the solar array but didn't find him, and then to their bunk, which was empty, and then back to the tower where the dead were wandering near the flames.

And there was Todd with screaming, writhing Chloe.

She tried to take the baby from his arms, but he wouldn't let her. He nodded to the rifle. "You're better than me."

Then he pulled her for the far tower, the one still standing, and when they got cut off, and they knew they'd have to make it up and over, Emily once again tried to take Chloe away.

"I'm stronger."

She shook her head violently. "Let me."

"Go, Emily."

Behind them, the dead were coming, slowly. Even though they had lost themselves, they knew there was no reason to rush in for the meal. Emily was halfway up the fence when she felt it shake and Todd fell.

And Chloe screamed.

"Christ," she whispered, but she didn't know if she was swearing or praying.

The barbwire ripped her arms to pieces as she reached for them both. The barbwire sliced chunks from her jeans.

"Christ." It seemed like all she remembered how to say.

Todd flew at the fence. He fell.

And the dead had made it to him. She slid down the fence as fast as she could make it, slid the rifle around and up into the pocket of her shoulder, and did her best to keep them away, but there were so many.

And she couldn't fire faster. She couldn't hit Todd or Chloe. Todd finally leapt, his grip held, and he was just out of reach. There was a second, a look that passed between them when they thought they'd be okay, in between one shot and the next, one slow breath and another.

Todd dropped Chloe.

Emily screamed and tried to crawl down the fence, but the barbwire held on, unencumbered by the baby, Todd climbed up faster than she could climb down. He ripped her from the barbed wire, and they fell down the other side, watching, withered from the ground behind the fence as Chloe came apart like a doll in the frenzy of the dead. She was wailing, then gone, in a second that seemed like years.

Emily tried to climb again, knowing that it wouldn't do any good; she didn't care. She didn't care about anything.

Every moment she was forced to live filled her with darkness, like her body was cold and her face was black with poisoned veins. She didn't know how long she'd wept and screamed, but she remembered Todd clamping a hand over her mouth, dragging her into the woods.

They could still smell the smoke for miles when Todd stopped to catch a breath and lean back against a tree. There were tears in his eyes. He cared that much at least. She wanted to pull up the rifle and kill them both, to punish him, and to end her pain. But it was too hard to do anything but crumble and bleed.

"I want to go home." She said when he wrapped his arms around her again. He'd done what she'd asked but didn't realize they were thinking of home as two very different things.

25

There was a knock at the nursery room door. "Emily? It's me."

"It isn't locked." She wiped her face on Chloe's blanket. Emily felt like her voice was coming from someone else's throat.

Red stirred from her side. He'd been laying down, keeping off his injured leg, but he was up the second the door opened, and limping between Todd and Emily, growling, and showing his teeth.

"Is the dog, okay?"

"He'll live." Red chomped at the air and snarled in Todd's direction.

Emily pulled her eyes up to Todd's face. He still looked tired, like his eyes were sinking into his skull, and pushing out his veins. Todd tried to sit down on the floor, but he collapsed half way. "Don't let him kill me, Em. Please."

"He doesn't have to. You're dead already. He's been trying to tell me for days."

Todd nodded and managed to sit up against the wall. "I'd rather not be dog food, if you think that's okay."

"Red. Come." The dog returned to her, and Emily got him to lay down again with great difficulty. "How long since you've been bitten," she said, the smell of Chloe still clinging to her face. "By the look of you, I'd say two or three days."

Todd nodded again.

"How did it happen?"

"The cashier at the store. It's been so long I can't remember his name."

"The zip tie didn't hold him?"

"Nothing holds forever, I guess."

"Were you going to tell me or just turn and rip me apart, because it's too late for that. I'm already in pieces."

"I was going to tell you. I'd never have let myself hurt you."

"You hurt me every day."

"I would have told you." He stared at the carpet and plucked at a few strands of it with his fingertips.

"Bullshit. Always bullshit. You would've kept it secret to the last, and maybe killed us both. You're that selfish, and it's too late for you to change."

"I'll change enough." Todd's voice was heavy. "And that will finally make you happy."

"Oh yes. Your great sacrifice. Thanks." She huffed. "It won't make me happy, Todd. Nothing you do could ever make me happy again. Now, it's just easier to walk away."

"You'll go to the others, I suppose."

"Yes, with the others. They're not like last time, Todd. They helped me and asked for nothing in return, unlike you."

"So, you remember then."

"I remember all of it."

"Then you remember I tried to help you. I tried to save you and. . ."

"Chloe, Todd. You're such a coward you can't even say her name."

"You two were all I wanted. I just realized it too late."

"I was never what you wanted. I was never who you wanted. The only way you could love me was for me to pretend, to constantly put on a play for you. To make you dinner and take care of the house and let you feel like a king. And even then, you didn't want me. Not really."

"Of course, I did, Em. You're everything."

"I'm everything you should have wanted."

He was too sick to give her anger, so he only showed her pain. "I protected you. I kept you safe."

"You protected me." She felt a rush of sadness for him, but it passed as quickly as it came. "I only needed to be protected because you were so convinced I was weak, you made me believe it too. This world of lies you built, you didn't make it for me. It was always for you. You knew the only way you could keep me was to cut me off at the knees."

"It isn't true."

Emily stroked Red, who was still intent on showing Todd his very sharp teeth. "Believe what you want. Apparently, I don't care enough to lie to you." She left him then, splayed out on the floor of the nursery sweating himself to death and letting the darkness inside him spread through every vein.

She packed a bag of little things. Not only clothes, but memories. A picture of her parents, the picture of herself and Danny. There were no pictures of Chloe, so she took a little onesie with pink hearts and flowers in neat rows.

Todd looked up at her as she folded it and put it in her bag. "Please. Don't leave me. I'm so afraid."

Emily sighed and sat down beside Todd on the floor. "Of what? Dying?"

"Losing you."

"Lie to me again, Todd. That'll help."

He drew a slow breath. "Of losing me."

Emily put both hands on the back of her head and pulled her fingers through her hair. Almost every piece of her wanted to leave him in a pile on that nursery floor, so his last thoughts would be of Chloe and loneliness, but she was only cruel in her brain.

Her heart remembered love. Her heart remembered looking into his eyes the first time they'd held Chloe, and seeing magic, and happiness, and peace. She did remember everything, and that meant she remembered the way he'd leaned in and kissed Chloe's head, and curled up beside them in the hospital bed to rest his head on Emily's shoulder and his hand over hers as she held Chloe.

He'd tried to save them all even if he failed. And whether he'd done it the right way or the worst way, he'd kept Emily alive long enough to remember all those lovely, happy things.

"Will you stay? Not because I'm afraid. I mean I am but, all this time, I remembered her alone. Just stay with me a little while, in this room, where we can be a family again for a few minutes before I die."

"It won't be like dying. Not really." She reached over and petted his wet hair and scooted closer to him to pull his head into her lap. "To die is to be forgotten."

"You won't forget me?"

"I won't forget you, Todd. I don't want to."

"So, we had something, at least."

"Something." She turned her face away and wiped her eyes with palm of the hand he hadn't claimed. "Sometimes, even something great."

"Sometimes."

She squeezed the hand he'd taken. "You don't have to suffer, Todd. If you want me to end it for you, I will."

"You've been wanting to kill me for years."

He tried to laugh, but that part of him had already died. "I'd rather suffer if it means you'll stay."

"I'll stay. But I won't stay in the dark." She reached behind them and pulled the curtains open as wide as she could reach. The evening sun was clouded by rain, but the pink light that reached through the clouds created a glow in the room that almost made it feel alive again.

They said nothing because there was nothing else either of them could say, and she stayed with him until the sunset turned to moonlight and watched him fade and grey. Sometime, a few hours before dawn he fell asleep. She knew he'd never wake, so she climbed out from under him and went to their room for a pillow to tuck beneath his head.

Red watched her, laying just outside the nursery doorway, his eyes never straying from Todd. "It's okay, boy. It's almost time. Everything will be okay."

It was after sunrise when he took his last breath, and Chloe's room was filled with light. She turned the lock on the inside, then stepped outside and closed the door.

She had to carry Red downstairs, and she left him on the sofa as she spent one last morning in her garden, taking all the food she could carry to the SUV to share with the others.

She watched the upstairs window, kissed by sunlight, with its green curling vine.

It wasn't long. She blinked as he appeared in the window frame, his handsome face streaked by puffy black veins. Almost a stranger, he looked down at her, his eyes bloodshot and vacant, and put his hand on the windowpane to say goodbye.

About the Author

Cheryl is originally from the Blue Ridge Mountains in North Carolina and Tennessee, but now resides in Phoenix, Arizona where she teaches English, listens to Chopin, and sings loudly when no one is looking, except her pet rats. She loves zombie history and anything made with salted caramel. She is also the author of *Blackbird and the Mirror*.

Keep up with her and upcoming books at
www.cloudermelt.com

www.ingramcontent.com/pod-product-compliance
Lightning Source LLC
Chambersburg PA
CBHW031721170626
46808CB00005B/1829